299

THE CHOSEN ONE

It was not a question of good or evil, right or wrong. That's what "they" would never understand. There was a way things had to be.

The last one had not understood any part of it, even when he explained it to her on the mountain road in the headlights. He had told her the whole story there while she stupidly cried and begged; told her how he was chosen, how he had been in Mexico and found the secret in the pyramids of the Aztecs, in the stones that had run with blood; told her how the chosen ones then had longed for it, longed to meet the knife, but she had heard none of it, she had felt none of the joy. . . .

She had felt only the edge of his knife.

NIGHT
RITUALS

by
GARY PAULSEN

BANTAM BOOKS
NEW YORK · TORONTO · LONDON · SYDNEY · AUCKLAND

This novel is a work of fiction. Names, characters, places and incidents are either the product of the author's imagination or are used fictitiously. Any resemblance to actual events, locales, organizations or persons, living or dead, is entirely coincidental and beyond the intent of either the author or publisher.

This edition contains the complete text
of the original hardcover edition.
NOT ONE WORD HAS BEEN OMITTED.

NIGHT RITUALS

A Bantam Book / published by arrangement with
Donald I. Fine, Inc.

PRINTING HISTORY

Donald I. Fine, Inc. edition published 1989
Bantam edition / January 1991

ISBN 0-553-28817-2

Published simultaneously in the United States and Canada

Bantam Books are published by Bantam Books, a division of Bantam Doubleday Dell Publishing Group, Inc. Its trademark, consisting of the words ''Bantam Books'' and the portrayal of a rooster, is Registered in U.S. Patent and Trademark Office and in other countries. Marca Registrada. Bantam Books, 666 Fifth Avenue, New York, New York 10103.

THIS ONE IS FOR RAY.

THE
SEED

She would make him what he was, give him all that he needed to become noble, sacred; she would give him the knowledge of women, of the power of women, the terrible power of them and she would open the places in him to receive the spirit, the true spirit of the Aztecs.

His mother.

In the beginning he hated her, his core hated her, his soul hated her because she made him feel wrong.

The first time she came into the darkened bathroom while he was masturbating, his hand on his penis. He looked up at her. There was light around her head, a glow that came from above, came from the gods.

He expected her to say something, yell at him, chastise him.

Instead she came forward, put her hand on his penis and moved it, slowly at first, still silent, then faster and faster until he could stand it no longer, until he released and messed her hand, his legs, his stomach and the wall.

Then she turned, still silent, and walked out of the bathroom, the light still shining around her head, wiping her hand delicately on a towel.

First time, and there was horror and hate.

After that she would wait until he was in the bathroom, either bathing or sitting on the toilet, and always she would turn the light off and come in with the light in back of her, the glow from the gods and put her hand on him until it became a ritual, a part of his life.

The ritual started in his fourteenth year and didn't end until he was seventeen when he first had sex with a young woman from school. His father was gone, divorced but considered to be dead by his mother, and they lived alone. After a time there came to be a look between them, a way he would glance at her when he got up to go to the bathroom, and she would follow and turn out the light and touch him there, touch him with the light in back of her head and finally, when he was nearly seventeen, she came to him one night when he was asleep and crawled into bed with him and took him inside of her. That night she made sound, a moaning and shuddering sound that came from the light from the gods. And he knew then he did not hate her any longer, nor hate any other women. He knew then they were sacred and that he was being chosen, chosen to seek the sacred women out. She came back to him many times at night, many times to take him inside and moan and shudder with him so that he would know he was the one, the one special person in all of time who was not wrong.

Special and chosen, although he didn't yet know for

what and would not know about being a prince until he was old enough and the voice came to him to tell him of the rituals of the Aztecs and what he must do.

For all of that time, until he was told by the spirits, he kept the ritual a secret. For his time in training and his time in work and his time in marriage and his time in life he kept it a secret but it was there, waiting, waiting, waiting . . .

The secret boiling beneath the surface, waiting for the right moment.

Waiting.

NIGHT
RITUALS

CHAPTER ONE

Milo Daimler hummed the new opening as he pulled his trash collection cart past the security gate. He nodded and smiled at Teresa who smiled back and gave him their private look that meant she was sick as hell of watching X-ray pictures of people's toilet articles. As he started out onto the E concourse of Denver's Stapleton International Airport, Milo thought of later that night. Later he and Teresa would drink a few beers and he would tell her about the new piece he was working on, a completely original work on the electric organ composed just for her, for them.

Stapleton was being modernized—they were always modernizing some part of the airport—and Milo had to work his way past the construction areas. As he did, he concentrated on the opening of his piece, which was everything. Since the last time he saw Teresa, he had bought a new Hammond electric organ with a complete built-in rhythm section and he was composing a love song for her. Well, not a love song he thought, pulling a trash sack out of one of the containers and dumping it into his car, so much as a lust song. He had been working at Stapleton in the custodial section for close to sixteen years and never once, in all that time, had he known a woman like Teresa. She was his age, forty, and she wore leopard skin bikini panties and had a flat stomach and came to his apartment and stayed on him until his left arm hurt and he had to take a hypertension pill.

Not only was she an animal in bed but she loved music as well and stood in back of him pushing her crotch against his bare back while he played the electric organ for her. And now, with the new organ and its complete rhythm section, he was composing a brand new piece that would be good enough even for a professional like Barry Manilow or Wayne Newton. He had the beat now, and the first part of the melody, and he hummed it again as he emptied another trash container into his cart, one practiced eye watching the trash slide over the lip. People threw away some pretty incredible stuff sometimes. Once he found a briefcase with a small computer inside, just dumped in the trash. And lots of times he found food. Not just scraps or leftovers but real food. Sometimes canned goods from foreign countries or whole loaves of sourdough bread, still in the wrappers, just jammed down into the trash cans whole. After sixteen years he always watched when he dumped and so he noticed the heft of the small overnight bag as it fell from the can into his cart.

The bag said ETRE on the side in bright purple letters, with a swatched line under the letters, and he thought he might give the bag itself to Teresa after he found out what was so heavy inside it. He looked at the waiting passengers to make sure none of them had seen the bag drop into his cart. He was at gate E-18, a Northwestern gate, and the passengers were too busy checking in to even notice him. One small boy was staring at him but turned away when Milo stared back.

He hurried off down the concourse, pulling the cart until he came to the small utility room next to the toilets. He used a key from the ring on his belt to open the door, and then made sure that Benny wasn't anywhere around. Benny was the wax man and a complete asshole and if he saw Milo with anything good he would want a part of it or he would turn Milo in to the supervisor, a cranky old bastard named Foxes who was just waiting to land on Milo because Milo got Teresa before he did.

Benny was gone and Milo locked the cubicle before flicking on the light. He could not figure out why the bag was so heavy. It had real heft to it as he pulled it out of the cart. From the outside, whatever was inside felt soft, but there was something to it as well, something familiar to his touch that he couldn't quite place. He fumbled with the zipper and jerked twice before he got the bag open; then he reached in and pulled the contents out, held it up and gagged.

In his hand was a rather large severed breast of a woman. Had Milo been able to consider it he would have seen that it was once a beautiful breast, perfectly formed, off a young white women who had been well endowed. But Milo wasn't thinking logically. The shock of seeing

3

the breast, holding it, the cut side facing him with bits of tissue hanging down, was too great, harder even than the bouncing of Teresa on top of him in the waterbed. He had one jolt of pain that started in the center of his chest and shot out and down his left arm, and then Milo was clinically as dead as the cut-off breast before he hit the floor.

CHAPTER TWO

Homicide detective Ed "Push" Tincker held up his hand for another beer but Scarf was arguing with a traffic cop down where the bar turned the corner. The argument was political. The traffic cop thought that the Supreme Court was getting more conservative and might someday actually start to think more of the cops and victims and less of the perps. Scarf, a retired vice cop who had bought this bar with his pension money, was advancing the subtle intellectual argument that the Old Farts would not be conservative until they allowed the cops to stretch the perps' scrotums over barrel heads before questioning, or better yet, instead of questioning.

Push leaned across the bar and drew a Coors for himself. Scarf caught the motion out of the corner of his eye and drifted down the bar to collect Push's money without losing the place in his argument. He never missed. This was a cop bar—as close to the mountains out on Colfax Avenue as Denver's western city limits could stretch—and cops were notoriously dishonest about paying for anything. They were always looking for ways to squeeze free drinks out of Scarf and they were never successful at it.

"It's like this," Scarf said to the traffic cop. "We're going to have to go way to the right to make up for all the *Miranda* bullshit, to even it out. I figure it will be about even when cops can blow perps up just for looking suspicious . . ."

Push carried his beer back to the quiet table in the rear by the picture of the horses. He liked the picture of the horses. There were four of them standing by a watering tank in the middle of the prairie and they looked so happy, standing drowsily in the hot sun. Push could almost hear them breathing, hear the buzzing of the flies around them, the plop of their turds hitting the ground— it made him serene to think of the horses.

The bar was relatively quiet because it was still early afternoon. But when it was time for these guys to begin the evening shift and the cops from the day shift came in and started to drink, the atmosphere would get rough and loud and physical and the bar would stink of puke. It was Friday night, the worst night of the week to be drinking in a cop bar. The only place possibly worse was a biker bar on a Saturday night. After a week of work the cops needed to unwind and Push liked to be serene and gone when they started. Last time he saw them unwind, an old traffic sergeant named Clinton came out of the john with a live chicken in one hand and his dick in the other and swore he was going to screw the chicken if he could get some-

6

body to cut the head off at the right moment so he could get the dying quiver. It had been a memorable evening for everybody except the chicken but it ended with shots being fired—three rounds from Clinton's service revolver through the front window when he tried to hit the chicken being held by the rookie who only wanted to be accepted by the oldtimers. Everybody later got caught up in the paperwork after some asshole had turned them in—one of the bullets went across the street and took a drink off a bar in front of some lush. Since then Push tried to get away before it got wild.

He thought of ordering one of Scarf's burritos—it was about dinnertime—but he was going to meet Rosa later and Scarf's burritos had a way of making his stomach detonate. They were good—Scarf said it was because he used real burro meat—but the green chilis were molten lead.

"Push—tell this goddam cherry how you got your name," Scarf yelled suddenly from the bar. "It's a good story . . ."

Push smiled but said nothing and Scarf turned back to the young cop who was sitting nursing a beer and probably wondering what he would tell his new wife when he got home with the booze on his breath.

"Push came off shift early one night and caught his wife getting tube from some asshole. So the guy doesn't see him, right? So Push goes quiet back out and sees the guy's car across the street—a brand new Trans Am. Right about then a street-cleaning truck comes by, you know the kind with the scoop on the front that lifts the dirt up over the top? So Push, he tells the truck driver what's up and lays a twenty on him and the driver lets Push use the truck. He locked the scoop on that frigging little Trans Am and started pushing it down the street. Only it turns sideways, right? So Push gets the scoop just right and keeps prodding it and the Trans Am starts rolling over and over like a dog or something, just over and over. Push rolled that car two blocks, just kept pushing it until it was totaled. And that's how he got his name."

The young cop looked over to where Push sat at the table and Push turned away. It was a good story but only partially true. It didn't tell of the rage he felt when he saw the man's back thrusting down and into his wife. His wife. His only wife. He could remember the muscles in the man's back, cording when he pushed, the man's ass sticking in the air . . .

He had drawn his revolver and aimed it, all in silence, and still—even when he was drunk and reliving the misery which he did about once a month—still he could not understand why he had not put the three pounds of trigger squeeze into his finger and killed the man on his wife. Just one squeeze separated the man from his death and he hadn't done it. Instead he had gone out, stumbling blindly, and seen the car and the car had become the man, the man's back and legs thrusting, the man himself and when the truck came by he had decided to kill the man-car, kill him and kill him and kill him . . . And so his nickname.

In the rough humor of the department, he became known as Push for what he did to the car. But he had really been killing, killing all that the man was or would be. It had been his own fault that she had gone outside the marriage; his neglect of her, the rough edges and calluses that came with his job, the turning away he had done when she reached out. But that didn't matter. He still killed the car and wanted to kill the man and would still like to kill the man.

Push looked back to the front door as another off-duty cop came in. He was a blond kid Push had seen around—they all looked like kids to him now that he was thirty-five—and Push stood to leave. Part of him wanted to stay and wolf down one of Scarf's burritos but it would kill Rosa. She said she didn't care, but he knew his eating without her bothered her.

He was halfway to the door when the phone rang. Everybody in the room paused, listening as Scarf picked it up. Every branch of the department knew Scarf's number and many of the cops gave Scarf's phone as their most easily reached off-duty point if there was an emergency. Not a few of them could be found at Scarf's more than at home with their families. Scarf lifted the phone to Push and held it out with his eyes raised in a question. If Push shook his head Scarf would say he wasn't there—Scarf was almost viciously loyal to his customers and had been known to lie to the chief and once even to the mayor.

Push shrugged and took the phone, leaned across the bar. "Yes." It was how he always answered the phone. One word, noncommittal. Safe. Now and then he caught a reprimand from the department because officially he was supposed to state his name and position but he had long ago stopped worrying about most procedures. Reprimands only mattered if you were concerned about your career in law enforcement. He didn't care about that. He was not sure just exactly what he did care about, if anything, but he knew he didn't care about his career in law enforcement. He'd like to get his pension, if possible, and now and then stayed within the rules for that reason. But he'd long ago given up on the idea of law enforcement; now he just tried to clean up the dirt and survive.

"Push, this is Dave. We got one."

"Where and what?" Push looked longingly as Scarf went by with a steaming burrito for somebody else down the bar. Dave Thorsen was his sometime-partner, a tall, thin, sad-looking man who was married and had two children who loved him. Dave hated every moment he was away from them. Usually Push worked alone as a senior homicide detective, preferred it, but if a case came that took two he would work with Dave. They weren't partners in the true police sense of the word—which was almost a blood relationship—but sometimes they worked together and they were very close.

"It's a weird one out at Stapleton."

Push winced. He liked his homicides to be predictable—no mysteries. Family conflict, suicide, anger flashing up and somebody getting killed. He hated the weird ones. They always complicated things. "Tell me."

Dave laughed on the phone. "A janitor holding a tit was found dead in one of those custodial rooms."

"A tit? You mean he died holding a woman?"

A snort. "No. Just the tit. A cut-off tit. Wait until you see it. I'm out here now calling from a pay phone."

Push hesitated, letting the information sink in, then let out a huge sigh. "Which concourse?"

"Out on E—near gate E-18."

"I'm on the way." He hung up, nodded to Scarf and went out the door into the smog-stink of a Denver evening. It was getting dark and he could see the mountains outlined against the setting sun. They looked like cardboard cutouts in the yellowish air. The department Dodge had air conditioning but it had never worked so he rolled the windows down as he pulled out into the traffic on the street.

He picked up speed and moved through the cheap motels and dumpy bars that marked Colfax—glaring lights, grubby bars with hookers working like tired wolves looking for sheep. Push liked Colfax. It was down and dirty and honest. You knew you could get your ticket punched on Colfax. You expected it. Nothing phony about it. The hookers called it AIDS Alley.

Push turned off Colfax onto I-70 and kicked it up to eighty. Might as well play the game. He took the light out of the under-dash bracket and put it on top of the dash and left it there as he turned off the interstate and into Stapleton Airport. He parked in the departure lane, left the light on top but took the keys and locked the car. It was not unusual to get police cars stolen, even at the airport. Hell, especially at the airport.

Inside he headed straight for the E concourse, flashing his badge at a sharp-edged looking woman as he went through security and rode the walkway for what seemed like an hour before he finally saw the sign for gate E-18 ahead. Passengers moved past in a normal flow and he didn't see the crime scene tapes until he was right next to a hallway that had been roped off. Two uniform cops were there—he knew them both and nodded to them—and four airport rent-a-cops. There were also three men dressed in suits standing next to the door to a closet.

Push guessed they had something to do with airport administration. He ducked under the tape and went to the door, ignoring the suits and the rent-a-cops. Like all police he had an automatic mistrust of any hired security force and an equal mistrust of administration. Any administration. In the small cubicle he saw Thorsen, an almost gentle, pensive look on his face, looking down at a corpse—as if Dave expected the body to say something to him.

Push nodded and squatted by the head of the body. The face was contorted with pain and rigor mortis had set in. The body was on its left side, the left arm out and the head resting on it. One foot was mashed against the wall, the other toed in at an odd angle that meant the man was probably dead when he hit the floor. The room smelled of urine and feces—along with blood the most common smell at a homicide location. In the left hand was a bag with ETRE on the side. The right hand still gripped the cut off breast of a woman.

"You weren't kidding, were you?" Push leaned over to look at the breast more closely. "Nice shape to it . . ."

"I called the M.E. and the meat wagon is also on the way," Thorsen said.

Push nodded once more. "Good. But I don't want to move the body before we get good pictures and I can place the crime scene in my mind." If it was a crime, he thought. The contorted face probably meant a heart attack and the breast could mean anything. But in this situation you followed procedures all the same, even if you didn't believe in them. "We should check the bag and the breast for prints other than the dead man's and then maybe get to the medical school at the university. Also we might check the hospitals. This has all the earmarks of some medical student pulling a prank."

Thorsen nodded, writing in a small notebook. "Some prank. Killing the poor son of a bitch, I mean. He must have reached in the bag and bought it when he pulled out the tit."

Push said nothing but agreed with Thorsen. He looked around the room once, then again, studying everything. Brooms in one corner, a rolling vacuum, some naked lady pictures on the wall over a sink. No signs of violence—just a dead janitor holding a tit. He turned to the door. Had to face the bastards. He went out to where the three men in suits still stood waiting.

Incredibly, impossibly, there were no reporters yet. This was a made-to-order news item—poor taste, grossness, sensationalism with sexual overtones. He should be beating them off with a club and there were none of them. One of the suits moved away from the other two and approached Push.

"I'm Stanton, Michael Stanton. I'm with administration . . ."

Surprise, Push thought—I figured you for another janitor. "Do you have any ideas about what happened yet?"

Push shrugged. "I was going to ask you the same question. Who found the body?"

"A child walking by—he smelled the odor coming from . . . him . . . and told his parents who called security because they thought some wino had used the cubicle for a bathroom. They're sitting out in the waiting area of gate E-18." He leaned closer to Push. "This might seem callous but I hope that we can keep this relatively quiet. The airport doesn't need this kind of publicity."

Push said nothing. A trick he'd learned years before. Don't say anything unless you specifically had something to state. He had started using this trick when questioning suspects—was amazed at how many of them took silence to mean knowledge and would rattle on and on and often give themselves away. Sometimes when Push didn't even suspect them—back when he was new.

Now he suspected everybody of everything. It made it all easier. He turned away from Stanton. Now it was all procedure. The same procedure for all homicides. Gather as much evidence as possible, get pictures, memorize the scene, get prints from everything and everybody, get statements from everybody in the area—gather it all and then set to work, sifting, checking and sifting and sifting and rechecking. Procedures. Push sometimes found comfort in the procedures, a predictable comfort. He hated a mystery, as all cops did, and the procedures had a way of evening the mysteries out.

He and Thorsen started the procedures now. Check the fingers of the dead man, look for scars or marks that might mean a fight; check the body closely, look for any signs of entry—Push had seen a man killed with a needle in the back of the head, up into the brain, and it hadn't shown up until a sharp doctor caught it in the autopsy. Look under the body, in every corner of every inch of the room.

Procedures.

Push looked at his watch and sighed. It would be midnight, easily, before he got done with the crime scene. He would have to call Rosa and tell her he was going to be late.

He wished he had eaten one of Scarf's burritos.

Push looked at the ceiling. Outside on Colfax a neon sign went on and off and sent a green-yellow glow into the motel room. He took his watch from the nightstand next to the bed and held it in the glow to see the numbers. Four o'clock.

The street traffic had slowed outside but soon the delivery trucks would be starting to move. Next to him Rosa breathed evenly, smoothly. He studied her in sleep—something he seldom had the chance to do because he was usually asleep himself, exhausted by their lovemaking. Facing him, she breathed cleanly, gently, with no rattle, her breath moving against his cheek like a caress.

She was beautiful to him, with short dark hair and full lips, a rich body with full, delicately balanced breasts and a soft, round-flat stomach. Freckles showered down her throat onto her breasts and he could not think of her without becoming aroused. Even in sleep in the red glow, with her mouth slightly open, she was beautiful and he could not believe she liked him, could not believe how they had met and had somehow come together. She'd had a flat tire at the airport. He'd been there on a case and stopped to help her; there had been talk, a drink, and some incredible force had drawn them together so strongly he did not understand it then and still did not.

He was stocky, built like a fireplug, would someday be bald, and she was the type of woman he thought of as golden—a golden woman. She made love with an almost tragic, longing intensity; a soaring hunger that made her convulse in multiple orgasms that were so focused they sometimes frightened him. They seemed to take her near the edge of death. It was as if each climax could make up for all the climaxes she had never had in her successful, sterile marriage. She rarely spoke of her marriage, her husband who was a pilot, but on one occasion she said with bite in her voice that he was "exactly perfect. Like a molded Ken doll." Push had gotten the impression he was not good in bed, was not inventive. But she didn't say that other than to imply it with her hunger, her great hunger for all things sensual. "You don't care," she told Push once after they had nearly torn a motel room to pieces. "You don't care what you do—you just do everything, don't you?"

Another look at his watch—four-thirty. Rosa had to get up at five to get showered and made up before meeting her husband at the airport. He flew for Pan Am and she had to pick him up at six to drive him up to their home in Evergreen—an expensive, arty, small bedroom community in the mountains west of Denver.

Push felt his stomach tighten, looking at the curve of her shoulder. If he awakened her a little early they could make love again. He ran his fingers across her breast, fondled the nipple, and she opened her eyes and smiled, stretched and arched her back.

"What time is it?"

"Four-thirty. I thought we might want to wake up a little early . . ."

She raised up over him and kissed him, letting her tongue work into his mouth, using her hands on him until he was fully hard, then taking him into her and starting to move, pushing her wetness down on him. He moaned and followed her movements, holding her hips with his hands, rising to her and at that moment the phone rang.

"What the hell?" She stiffened, rolled off him.

He hesitated. The only person with this number was Dave Thorsen—he had to leave a number with somebody in case of an emergency—and Dave would not call unless it was vital, a true emergency.

He held Rosa with one hand, grabbed the phone. "Yes."

"It's me." Thorsen's voice was strained. "They called me at home and woke me. You'd better come in. I'll meet you at the office."

"What's the matter?"

"They found another tit . . ."

"Where?"

"Seattle."

"Seattle? You mean Washington?"

"Yeah—but they think it came off a flight originating in Denver. You know what I think?"

17

Push said nothing, waiting. He suspected what Thorsen was about to say.

"I think we got a cutter on our hands."

"Yes, I'm coming. Half an hour."

Push hung up and exhaled. He put his hand on Rosa's breast but it was clearly not to be. She sat up, picked up her bra from the floor and put it on, straightened the straps. "Christ, it must be awful being married to you."

He studied her back for a moment, then sighed. "Yes. It was."

Please, he thought, almost a prayer as he rolled to the right and found his pants. Please don't let this be a cutter.

CHAPTER
THREE

Cutters.

It had happened in 1979. Push was new to homicide, coming from vice. Years of busting hookers and popping numbers drops, closing down late bars and tapping out the sex shows—years of worthless work, cop work for nothing. At least that's how Push felt. He would work undercover for a month, close down a floating game or numbers operation and the punks would be out on the street working again before he made it to the parking lot.

He called it Sillycop Work and because he was always late working on cases, usually drinking—or pouring drinks in rubbers to use as evidence of a bar serving late—his wife wandered from the marriage. It was then he decided that homicide was the only true police work. It was the only crime that could not change—to take a life, end a life. There was a kind of purity to it. Usually if the courts found the criminal guilty, he would get a significant amount of time. Push thought it might be the only way he could stomach staying on the force.

In a series of drunk nights at Scarf's, Push had carefully and logically worked it out with Scarf's help. He applied for a transfer to homicide and in the first week they popped his cherry.

He had been one of two cops in the office when the call came in, his first cutter. The other cop was dead now—a guy named Packard who smoked three packs a day but still looked surprised when told his lungs were gone. Packard had been a tough cop of the old school—what they called mean and down—from when a beat was the same as a turf, almost a small country, and the cop was head of a feudal fiefdom. Packard had, almost literally, owned people—moved the street people in his beat as if they were pieces in a giant chess game—and he had an air about him that many of those older cops had come to use: that of a king. In some strange way the aura followed them always, affected even their relationships with their superiors so that higher officers held them in respect and some fear. In that time before *Miranda,* before many controls existed, they were the law. All of it. In serious crimes the perp simply didn't get to court unless the beat cop wanted him to—it was easy to arrange accidental deaths and nobody dared question the police—and Push believed, as many cops did, that in some ways it was better then. Crime was more controlled then, was not as loose.

Push had been a cop long enough not to be surprised. At anything. Vice work was often as hard as any police work—he had seen the core of the rotten, or thought he had. Children bought and sold for sex, incest turned into a parlor game. All of it. But Packard was far beyond that state, had been working homicide for so long that it was part of him somehow. He was thick with it, with the smell of death—toughened and calloused so deeply that it was difficult to draw a line where the crime ended and Packard began.

When the call came they were eating and Packard signaled Push to bring his lunch with him in the car.

"We'll finish on the way," he had growled, his throat perpetually raw from the cigarettes. "It's a motel out on Colfax . . ."

It was the height of the livestock mutilation period, when satanist cults were cutting up range cattle to get the reproductive organs for their rites. Ranchers in eastern Colorado were forming auxiliary police units, patrolling sectors, trying to stop the cults. Close to two hundred cattle had been killed and cut in the prairie pastures and nobody had been caught. There were rumors that two killings in Colorado Springs were mutilation killings— two hookers were cut up in some motel rooms—but they found it was a fight between two pimps establishing territory. The pimps were offended that anybody cared about the hookers enough to make an investigation out of it.

In the middle of the mutilations Packard and Push got the call and went to the Cactus Motel. It was the smell that alerted the room clerk. She had come by in the afternoon, after the cleanup maid had gone and the room had been rented to " . . . one of them you know—one of the dark ones." Push wasn't sure exactly what she meant but it didn't matter. She had caught the smell from the

21

door as she walked by, the unmistakable smell that Push came to know as the crime scene smell. It was the smell of blood, a hot-rich smell so thick it stuck in his throat, choked him no matter how often he encountered it.

This first time the smell stopped him cold at the door. Packard pushed the door open—it wasn't locked—and stepped easily, almost casually into the darkened room. As though he were paying a call. In one hand he held his half-eaten sandwich. Push stopped at the door and gagged, caught his breath. He had seen a small boy once, anally raped, bleeding down his legs and crying into his soul, and he dreamt often of the boy's legs, white with the dark lines running down them—it was one of the recurring nightmares he had—but he had never thought he would see anything like what he saw in the Cactus Motel room.

He assumed it had been a woman—so many of them were women. Parts of her, including the primary section of the torso, lay on the bed but it was impossible to say even that it had been a human. All extremities were cut off, as were the breasts, and the body had been completely, almost clinically eviscerated. They found the arms and legs and entrails in the bathtub and the head in the toilet—and the walls were covered with hand smears of blood, lined in symbols that made no sense and the letter *F* scrawled repeatedly.

"Son of a bitch must have used an axe," Packard said, almost casually looking around the room, "or a saw of some kind. Never seen one like this before."

He then took a bite of the sandwich and Push lost it

all, vomited in an almost flat trajectory. He tipped back to the door, nearly falling, slipping on the blood on the floor—he could not then nor still believe the quantity of blood in the human body. A river of it. Somehow he got outside, leaned against the wall in the sun, took deep breaths, kept thinking oh-god-oh-god-oh-god.

The manager kept trying to see into the room without actually getting too close, ignoring Push's retching. "Pretty bad, huh?"

And all Push could think of was the sandwich in Packard's hand, the way he took a bite in the thick-smell middle of all the gore. To be that hard, so far beyond human. He could not believe that he would ever be that way and even later, when it happened and he became a Packard clone and had the same smell about him, the smell of death, he could not believe what he had experienced that day.

Push did not sleep that night at all, slept only an hour the next night, awakening in the damp nest of his bed, and he would never sleep a full night again, tired or not tired, not even after making love to Rosa when it worked right and there was nothing left of him. Always in the night he would awaken to lie in the dark and think. He would not always have nightmares, but whenever he awakened to lie that way, staring at the ceiling, there would come the thought of Packard's sandwich, the goddam sandwich.

Even now, he thought, even now that he had seen it all, all the horrors there were, seen all the horrors twice and many of them worse than that first time—even now he thought of the sandwich and at night the question would come. Always the question. He had never asked Packard and now it bothered him each night like a rash that would not go away.

What kind of sandwich had it been?

What kind of sandwich could he stand there and eat? Cutters.

He drove easily this time, his eyes burning from the lack of sleep, his stomach aching from the intense bouts with Rosa. It was past dawn but the sun wasn't up yet. He kept the window down, propped his elbow on the window and leaned back. It was too early for McDonald's but he stopped in an all-night grocery and got two large cups of black coffee, one with a lid. In the car, driving again, he drank one of them almost immediately, so hot it made his eyes water.

Then he popped the lid and sipped the second one more slowly, letting the caffeine jolt him alive. He had heartburn—an occupational hazard for cops, along with high blood pressure, suicides, heart attacks, obesity, bad backs and fallen arches—and he let the coffee fight down the heartburn, swallowing repeatedly until he got to the Denver central police station.

At one time, the station had been the tallest building in the center of Denver. Now it was dwarfed by the newer surrounding buildings. He saw Dave's car in the lot and parked next to it, went inside. It was, he thought for the ten thousandth time, amazing how ugly they made the station. Old, tacky, the plaster scratched and marked.

They had painted it again and again, one coat on top of the next, always a light institutional green that Thorsen had once called avocado-puke. The ceilings were tired tile with buzzing fluorescent fixtures, and the gray metal desks in the squad room were set in unimaginative rows.

Cockroaches moved with experienced courage in broad daylight from desk to desk looking for the inevitable crumbs of fast-food left by the detectives. At most of the desks were old typewriters, and they all seemed to be covered with crumpled bits of paper and sacks that had once held take-out food. The room smelled of urine and vomit—from the detention cage at one end—and sweat and an almost indefinable stale odor that to Push seemed to come from soiled underwear left in a hamper too long. It was a mix-odor, not one he could pin down, but one he sometimes got in laundromats and from his socks.

There was an equipment room where he left his gun—no guns allowed in the squad room since one fateful day when a drug addict completely ripped on speed got hold of a detective's .38 and turned the place into a free-fire zone. The addict had fired six times while men dived under their desks. He hit nothing except the coffee machine, a blessing in disguise for which the department felt he ought to be given a decoration.

At the other end was a door leading to a hallway off of which were four interrogation rooms, small cubicles used for questioning suspects or holding conferences. Two of the rooms had one-way mirrors and tables in the middle surrounded by metal chairs. One of the rooms had a fan mounted high up in one corner. The interrogation rooms smelled worse than the squad room—if that were possible—and the detectives hated to use them. Thorsen sat at a desk next to the doorway leading to the interrogation rooms.

"How's Rosa?" he asked. Push shrugged. "All right. Pissed because you called but there you are."

"There you are." Thorsen knew all about Rosa, as he knew all about Push's divorce and the real reason for his nickname, the rage he had held. He had held Push when he was drunk and crying, sobbing over his lost life and marriage. He knew Push's dreams, his soul—he knew all of Push's life as Push knew all about his. Within the department there were few secrets and between partners, even partners as loosely connected as Push and Thorsen, there were none. Thorsen knew that Push could not sleep, knew about the way Rosa reached climaxes, just as Push knew that Thorsen was becoming impotent on more and more occasions and was seeing a shrink for it. No secrets.

"What have we got?" Push sat at the desk next to Thorsen's, felt his butt stick to the seat and rose to see a piece of gum stuck to his pants. He scraped it off and sat down again.

"We have a pair of breasts, Caucasian, perhaps matching, one in Denver and one in a bag in Seattle."

"Why do they think the Seattle breast came from Denver?"

"You're not going to believe this." Thorsen pushed a piece of paper across the desk. "There was a name and address on the bag."

"Shit." Push took the paper. "James Matherson. 505 Circle Drive, Aurora, Colorado." He shook his head Aurora was a suburb about fifteen minutes from where they sat, if the traffic was light. "Could it be this goddam easy?"

Thorsen shrugged. "Remember Kloepnick . . ."

Harris Kloepnick was a junky who walked in one day, sat on the edge of Thorsen's desk and confessed to three homicides that had been in the open file for over a year— a nice way of saying they were probably not going to be solved. People came in and confessed to crimes all the time. They confessed to crimes that hadn't even been committed. Sometimes they confessed to crimes they just wished they had committed, hoping that the confession would make the crime happen in their minds. They were all crazy. But rather than throw Kloepnick out—the normal reaction—Thorsen acted on a hunch and dug the files out and asked Kloepnick trick questions. Kloepnick knew all the answers. He had killed the people during burglaries while trying to get money for his nose. And still more rare, when he got a lawyer and his lawyer told him to remain silent, Kloepnick waived his rights and did the confession again with witnesses, on tape, and actually signed the transcript. Thorsen had gotten a promotion out of it and Push had received a letter of commendation—all because a junky sat on the corner of Thorsen's desk.

"So let's bust him . . ."

They stopped at the equipment room and got assault gear, vests and shotguns, plus their handguns. It was five-thirty in the morning and they made good time in Push's car—Dave hadn't gotten one from the motor pool. Thorsen drove because he hated Push's driving, said it made him nervous. They didn't argue about it any longer but in the past Push had often driven anyway and would make a point of driving badly, cutting corners, following too closely, running lights. Thorsen would white-knuckle it until he couldn't stand it any longer, then reach over and pull the key and they would argue it out. Thorsen would talk sensibly, explain his fears, and Push would nod and smile and then do it again. Partners. Often worse than old married couples.

While they drove, Push loaded the shotguns, jacked rounds into the chambers and put them on safety. Homicides were usually "cold" crime scenes with the victim dead and the perpetrator long gone or sitting there in shock waiting to be arrested. And homicide arrests were almost always nonviolent. Vice, on the other hand, with drug busts and surprise raids through locked doors were often "hot" busts—prone to violence. You always went in ready in a vice bust. Many officers carried illegal loads, hollow points or dum-dums under the hammer, so the first load would put a perp back and down. Old habits died hard and Push put shells in the chambers on both shotguns, flicked them to safety, then grabbed the mike and ordered backup. He also ordered priors on Matherson, James, one each.

The dispatcher had three available and Push took them all. He gave the dispatcher the address, told them to come in quiet—he didn't want to awaken Matherson if he was asleep—and added for them to hold at the entrance of Circle Drive.

"Going to be a hot day." Thorsen drove evenly, not hurrying. He always made a show of not being nervous when they went to make an arrest. It was a thing with him because he knew Push would get more and more hyper the closer they got to the bust. The dispatcher came back to tell them there were no priors on Matherson, not even a traffic violation or parking ticket.

Push snorted. "The bust sucks, you know that?"

Thorsen nodded. "A true thing. A true thing."

"Well, shit. When have we ever had it this easy?"

"Agreed."

"The name and address right on the bag? I mean come on, get real."

Thorsen nodded.

"It's all shit—the whole bust."

"You said that."

"I know."

"Am I getting hyper?"

"Yeah."

"So drive and shut up."

It took them less then twenty minutes to get to the entrance to Circle Drive and the three patrol cars were already there. Thorsen pulled up next to one of them and Push rolled his window down. "It's 505 Circle Drive. We've got a very iffy homicide bust so let's be careful. We'll make the bust and you guys watch the back and side in case he runs."

The patrol cars left and Thorsen drove into Circle

Drive. It was part of one of those new subdivisions where they had used only four basic house plans so that in a curved street you could actually look across the circle and see the duplicate of your home. Matherson's house was exactly half way around the circle, a house of all angles and planes and glass.

Thorsen stopped one door away. They got out of the car and walked to the house, holding the shotguns down at their sides. There was absolutely nothing moving up or down the street. They stopped at the front door.

"We could knock . . ." Thorsen hesitated.

"Shit."

They agreed on one thing completely. There was only one way to do a bust—by having complete control of the situation. Never give them time to think or do anything to hurt you. Never give them time to get ready.

Next to the door was a leaded glass panel. Push used the butt of his shotgun and nudged a panel of blue glass near the knob. It fell to the floor inside with a tinkle as it broke. He reached in and around and unlocked the door.

Inside the house was silent, darkened to a grayness by closed drapes. Directly in front of them was a hall opening, to the left a living room and going up the far side of the living room an open metal staircase that went along the side of the wall to another hallway.

"Dog?" Thorsen whispered. He feared dogs, the more so because he once did a door-kickdown arrest into a pair of insane Dobermans that left him with stitches on his stomach and his ass and the private knowledge that the only way to stop a Doberman was to drive a wooden stake through its heart. He swore one of the dogs was still chewing on his ass after he'd blown most of its head off with his shotgun.

They waited for a moment, listening, but there was no dog. In the silence they heard breathing from the hallway at the top of the stairway. Push nodded with his chin to the stairs, held the shotgun at the ready and led the way up. His breathing was getting faster now but there was no other external sign of his nervousness.

At the top of the stairs he stopped and Dave waited one step down. Two doors on the left, one open, one closed, and another one closed at the end of the hallway. Push tried the first door and it opened quietly to reveal a children's room with two sleeping small forms in beds. A brief glimpse of wallpaper with dancing bears or something, then on to the next door. Bathroom. Empty. With a small nightlight in the shape of Pluto.

His thinking came in jerks now, quick bursts of knowledge as he planned the next move. Master bedroom at the end of the hall. He turned the knob and opened the door silently, breathing through his mouth to stay quiet, his breath now coming in short, jagged rasps.

He turned the knob slowly, silently, and opened the door. To the left was a large bed and two sleeping adults. Man on the right—Matherson—and a woman on the left. It was exactly six o'clock and as they stood, holding shotguns, looking at the sleeping pair, an alarm clock on the nightstand began to buzz. Push jumped with the sudden noise and heard Thorsen barely suppress a giggle.

The man rolled over, smacked his lips, reached a

hand to the alarm to turn it off, then opened his eyes to see two strange men standing in his bedroom, facing his bed with readied guns.

"What the hell . . ."

Push held up his badge, let the shotgun barrel down. "James Matherson? We're the Denver police department. You're under arrest. Please get dressed."

"Arrest? What . . . ?"

Push raised his voice a bit—control the situation. "Please get dressed. You have to come with us."

Matherson rubbed his face but remained sitting in the bed, the sheets fallen around his waist. "I can't be under arrest. I've never done anything . . . "

And that, Push thought, is probably the truest thing the poor son of a bitch ever said.

The woman next to him slept on, her face mashed into the pillow, oblivious to the room, the sound, all of it. One of her breasts showed from beneath the sheet.

Push used the barrel of his shotgun to scoop a pair of shorts off a chair next to the bed and drop them in Matherson's lap. "Get dressed."

Another classic bust.

CHAPTER
FOUR

The medical examiner—a man named Garner—belched and Push could smell his breath across the metal examining table between them, past the microphone that hung down. Sauerkraut. Jesus, how could he eat sauerkraut and cut up bodies? He was a fat man, the kind of fat that looked as if it would stay dented if you pushed a finger in it. Push disliked the man but he could not decide exactly why. He was good at his job, if calloused, but then who the hell wasn't calloused? It came with the turf.

They stood in a large room that was always cold—kept cold to keep the bodies from spoiling—and damp with water running all the time in various sinks around the walls and through various drainage tables in different parts of the room. Push couldn't stand in the room without having to piss.

Thorsen was waiting outside. He hated autopsies and could not watch one or even be in the same room without becoming sick. It wasn't that Push liked them, but he could stand them and at least one homicide officer had to be present. Watching didn't usually bother him unless it was a child. He hated to see a dead child being cut up, especially when the initial, radical incisions were made.

Not that this was anywhere near a complete autopsy On the table between them were two breasts. Whether intentionally—medical examiners were known for their crude humor—or by accident the breasts were placed almost exactly side by side on the table, with the nipples up and the cut off portion down against the stainless steel of the tabletop.

"Nice set of tits." The M.E. grunted and smiled. "Too bad we lost the rest of the woman." He tweaked one of the nipples. "Are you excited, my dear?"

Push ignored him. He knew now why he disliked the man. He waited.

The M.E. poked at one of the breasts with a rubber-gloved finger. "You want it technical or straight?"

"Straight. I mean we don't even know if we have a homicide yet. It could be a medical student playing a prank or some damn thing." He knew that if he asked for the technical aspects of it the M.E. would snow him with a lot of information he couldn't understand and didn't want. "I need to know time of death, if they match, who it was, age—all of that."

The M.E. snorted. "Maybe you'd like her name too."

Push waited.

The M.E. changed his voice, made it more authoritative. He was, after all, a doctor talking to a goddam cop—Push could hear it in his voice. "First off, they are a definite match. Blood type B, positive. A Caucasian. Judging by the condition of the breasts she was young— probably about twenty-three or four and had never had a child. Correction, had probably never breast fed. There is no real evidence of any heightened mammary activity so I would guess that she had never had a kid. There is also no evidence of cancer and the breasts were not re- moved surgically—which limits the chance that some medical student is screwing around."

"What do you mean, they weren't surgically re- moved? Is that something you can tell?"

"There was no skin flap, as there might be in a radical mastectomy, conventional surgery—which isn't likely in a woman this young anyway. These breasts were lopped off with a long-bladed knife." He turned one of the breasts over on the table. The back looked like a gray-red cottage cheese mass, spongy. He poked with his finger. "See the long marks? Like little stepped lines? Those are cut marks, made by pushing and pulling a long-bladed knife."

"Long-bladed—you mean like a butcher knife?"

The M.E. nodded. "Something like that. Long, and very sharp. See how these cut marks are clean, not torn at all? That's because the blade was very sharp . . ."

"A straight-edge razor blade?"

He thought a moment, then shook his head. "No. The cuts are too long and even. It was a long-bladed knife, but very sharp, like I said. The way it came up in

35

steps, or layers, I would guess that whoever cut them held the breast and pulled up on it while cutting across with a sawing motion—back and forth like this." He held his hand flat, palm up, and moved it back and forth. "Lifting while he cut."

"He?"

The M.E. shrugged. "I just figured it would be a man . . ."

No, Push thought—some of them are not men. Some of them are women. Some of them are men and some of them are women and some of them are something else. Some of them are not human. "How long ago?"

Another shrug. "There are so many variables—temperature at time of death, position of body at time of death, ambient temperature since death . . ."

"Give me a ballpark idea."

"Really crude guess—it's been at least five, six days. No, looser than that. Between three and seven days. I'd say not under three, the way the decomposition has started to deteriorate the tissue, but nowhere over seven or they'd be broken down more."

"Five days . . .?"

"A guess. Yeah. Five is all right."

Push waited, looking down at the two breasts. They looked so . . . so forlorn. Lonely, lying side by side on the cold metal. He hated the victims, hated what happened to them more than anything. No part of them was joy. They were always sad. Even when they were whole, the homicide victims always had a sad look lying on the metal tables, being cut open like sides of beef. Their eyes were always open and they always looked lonely and sad. Shit.

It could still be a prank. "Do you know anything else about her?"

The M.E. had a smug look. "I know it wasn't a medical student jacking off."

"How?"

The M.E. took a long-bladed scalpel and deftly cut one of the breasts in half through the nipple. "See the lividity? See how the line of blood has drained down towards the base?"

Push nodded. "I see the line—what does it mean?" But of course he knew the answer. He had to know the answer.

"If the breast had been cut off a corpse it wouldn't have that lividity line."

"She was alive when the breasts were cut off . . ."

The M.E. nodded. "Definitely. Her heart was still beating. She might have been unconscious, but she was alive."

Of course, Push thought, looking at the table. Of course she was still alive. There's no tooth fairy, Santa Claus eats Bambi, and she was alive when the asshole cut her breasts off. Jesus. A cutter. Oh Jesus.

Outside in the lounge Thorsen was waiting. Push brought him up to date, left out cutting the breast down the middle. That was the sort of thing that bothered Thorsen ever since the autopsy of the little girl. The impotency started then. She had been found in a dumpster and unlike many molestation cases there was not a mark on her. Aside from garbage there were no stains and her dress wasn't wrinkled and she had looked like Thorsen's daughter—or almost. Thorsen had hovered over the ambulance men when they lifted her out, and he had reached down to straighten her dress and a strand of her hair that had dropped over one eye. He had followed the body to the morgue and crossed the line and become personally involved. In that mood, thinking of his daughter and the molested girl, he had gone to the autopsy. When the initial cut was made, the radical cut across the chest and down the abdomen, he had hit the medical examiner so hard the doctor had required bridgework. Then the impotency had come.

"So we've got a cutter," Push finished. "No way around it."

Thorsen started for the door. "I called missing persons while I was waiting. There are four women missing in the last two weeks in Denver."

"Only four?" Push caught up. "A bad week . . ."

"That's what they said. There were more than four—some kids, a couple of young girls—but only four women. Three of them were black, one of them white."

"The breasts were from a white woman. Maybe twenty-four, plus or minus a year or two."

"I know. So I checked the name out. Betti—with an *i*—Fencer is the woman's name. She's been missing for six days. Didn't show up at work and she's not in her apartment. At least she doesn't answer the phone." They were at the parking lot next to the hospital that held the pathology department the city used for forensic autopsies. Thorsen rolled the driver's window down before he got in. He hated to sit in a hot car.

"What is her work?"

"She's a stewardess."

"Ahh"

"Yes. Ahh."

"Both breasts were found in airports."

Thorsen nodded in silence.

"Of course it could be another Matherson lead."

"Of course."

Matherson had lost his luggage when he foolishly checked all his bags on a trip to New York. He had turned in a lost luggage voucher and was waiting to be paid for the lost items—one of them a small bag that fit the description of the bag that had held the breast in Seattle. The whole arrest had taken on all the aspects of a bad dream. They had let Matherson go, naturally, when it became apparent that he was really innocent. At first he had seemed simply grateful to be gone—too grateful, really, Push thought. There had to be something there But apparently his wife, who had decided to get involved, talked to him on the way home and they had gotten a lawyer and were now going to sue for wrongful arrest. Chief of detectives, a mayoral ass-sucker named Quinsey, was threatening to make drumheads out of the skins on Thorsen's and Push's ass—his favorite expression.

"The thing with that Matherson business," Thorsen said, starting the car, "is that if it had gone the other way we'd be heroes."

Push looked out the window. A young woman with long legs jogged down the sidewalk. "I like summer. They're all out in tank tops and shorts and look so summery and fresh"

"We'd have been heroes and maybe gotten another commendation. Now all we get is shit on."

Push looked at him. "So what's the big deal? We'll handle it—just like always. This thing is really getting to you, isn't it?"

Thorsen said nothing for a moment, driving easily, then sighed. "Ahh, hell. It isn't this case. It's the thing at home."

"So what the hell, tell her it happens to lots of guys. They don't win the office football pool and they can't get it up—you know, lay it on her."

Thorsen shook his head. "Sue isn't making a problem out of it. You know, she understands and is always nice about it."

"Shit. That's worse . . ."

"Yeah. I mean if she bitched about it I could deal with it. But she's so nice and the goddam thing just hangs there."

"Have you been trying, you know, other ways?"

"Everything but a goddam Donald Duck suit. Christ, last night she put on these black garter things and stockings with one of those bras where you can see the nipples. I thought my blood pressure was going to tear off the top of my head."

"And no go?"

"Like a dead earthworm." Thorsen snorted. "It's like I'm looking down at somebody else's cock . . ."

He pulled up at the curb next to an apartment complex. "This is where Betti Fencer lives. It's a singles place."

"I knew we were going somewhere important."

"Apartment 310."

They walked up the three flights—Push noted that he was breathing hard by the second flight—and down a hallway to 310. The halls, the parking lot, the pool they could see through a couple of sliding glass doors in a courtyard in the back, the whole place was as deserted as a ghost town. Push smiled. A singles place in the middle of the day. They're all sleeping, waiting to party.

Thorsen knocked on the door. Repeated the knock several times. There was no answer.

"Let's get the manager."

Push nodded and they went back downstairs. I'll have to come back up again, Push thought—every step.

The manager opened the door widely—not the crack you would get in the inner city—and smiled at them. "Good afternoon."

He was tall, thin, wearing only a pair of purple briefs tailored for a bulging crotch, and had no hair on his chest or stomach. On top of his head were a pair of designer sunglasses, propped for effect—Push was certain he never wore them over his eyes—and he had apparently only recently come in from sunning. His body was covered with oil that shone in the backlight from the glass doors leading out to the pool and his voice had a phony low, husky quality on the edge of hoarseness.

"I was getting some rays."

Of course, Push thought—he had to be getting rays. He saw Thorsen's nostrils twitch, and he winced inwardly. Thorsen had an almost pathological hatred for

41

gays. It was something his shrink was working on and might have something to do with his impotence in some strange way—at least the hatred had gotten worse, if possible, since he became impotent. If he figured this guy was gay he might cork him.

"We're with the Denver police," Push started quickly. "We need to speak to Betti Fencer and apparently she's not in . . ."

"Well, you'll just have to get in line, won't you? I mean we all want to talk to little Bets, don't we? She's a week late on her rent and her little garbage deposit and she's always late, isn't she? I'm not surprised she's in trouble with the police. Honestly, Bets is just such a skitchy bitch."

"We want to get into her apartment," Thorsen said bluntly. His voice was like a snake coiling.

Oh shit, Push thought. He's brewing up.

"Well, don't we all want to get into the bitch's apartment? But I think we have to have a warrant or something, don't we?"

He's going to be cute, Push thought. He doesn't know how close he is to pulling his head out of his ass. Push stepped forward quickly. "Look—we're with homicide and we think Betti might be in trouble. We want to check her apartment to make sure she's not in there, or see if we can get an idea where she is. If you could help us we'd be very grateful."

"Or," Thorsen said, looming over the smaller man, "you could be difficult and I could kick your little ass until it's a ring around your little neck."

The manager studied Thorsen for a moment and saw his death in Thorsen's eyes. Push held his breath. It could go either way. It was not a time for the manager to show false courage. For a full second there was silence, then the man shrugged and turned. "Of course we can see her apartment. I'll get the spare key."

He put a T shirt on, with a designer name across the front, and led them back upstairs. Push wheezed along behind them.

Betti Fencer's apartment looked as if everybody's idea of a stewardess lived in it. Empty. Clean. Waiting. Push thought immediately of his own apartment, so slovenly that Rosa would not meet him there for what she called their interludes. Dirty shorts under the coffee table, green and growing things in his sink, an icebox he was nearly afraid to open.

Betti didn't allow dirt. The apartment was spotless, literally. New stereo and VCR in a rack next to the glass door leading out to a balcony over the pool. Carpet vacuumed so thoroughly that it looked to be combed all one way. Modern prints on the walls; modern furniture with a large teddy bear sitting on one end of the couch. The kitchen had all the modern appliances ever made waiting on the counters to blend, bake, broil, mix, heat, cool or process anything edible. All clean, shiny.

"Miss Neat . . ." Thorsen mused. He'd forgotten about the manager, who had stopped at the doorway but watched them closely—more out of curiosity than caution.

Push nodded. "Somehow it figures."

He moved into the bedroom—a large single bed, neatly made, with a bookcase on one end. He checked the books without really expecting anything and was surprised to see a row of Second World War books. He looked closer and at one end there were two romance novels. He pulled out one of the war books and flipped through the pages, was putting it back when he noticed some penciled writing on the back page.

"This book belongs to Jerry Brickner," he read aloud.

"Good old Jerry." Thorsen paused before entering the bathroom.

"You know Jerry Brickner?" Push turned to the manager in the doorway.

The manager shook his head. "Betti doesn't do much around here with anybody. She's very close. Actually rather snippity about it. I invited her down for drinkies once or twice but she never came."

Drinkies—Jesus. Drinkies. No wonder she didn't come. Push almost smiled. She was up here with Jerry Brickner playing Rommel does Africa—too busy to come down for drinkies.

Thorsen came out of the bathroom and shook his head. "Nothing but some cosmetics. She must have taken things with her."

They looked for anything to make the woman come alive for them. That was the basic premise in any homicide investigation—the victims had to come alive for the investigating officers. Hunches had to be followed as well as facts. Basic rules. Procedures. A network of life had to be manufactured to show what the victim had been like.

And Push knew without speaking that Thorsen had the same feeling he did. Betti had been the owner of the breasts. There was of course still some doubt and in a textbook investigation such a leap of judgment wouldn't be followed. But they were both street cops and knew one thing more than all the rest—coincidence simply didn't happen. The mathematical odds were too much against it.

The breasts were found in airports.

Betti had been a stewardess and she was missing, had been missing about the same time as the breasts had been separated from their owner.

Coincidence.

The problem was with her apartment. It was so clean, so sterile that it gave almost no indication of the person who lived there. They had a name—Jerry Brickner—but little else. There were no pictures, either of Betti or anybody else, no dirty cigarette butts, no used sanitary napkins, no garbage of any kind. A blank space, Push thought, waiting to be signed. He turned to the manager.

"Did she have any friends that you knew about? Any names at all you could give us?"

The manager shrugged, shook his head, pointedly ignoring Thorsen who now stood watching him as well. "As I said, she didn't socialize much around here. I believe she was friendly with Kate, but that's about it."

"Who is Kate?"

"Kate Driscoll. She's another stew who lives across the hall. I think she's home if you want to speak to her. I saw her come in this morning." He motioned to a closed door in back of him, on the other side of the hallway.

Thorsen shouldered past him, Push at his side, and knocked on the door. It took several moments but at last they heard the knob turn and a woman stood backlighted in a thin nightgown, obviously just awakened. Her hair was blonde and tousled and long and her eyes were a slanted green that lifted at the corners. Her figure, showing through the gown, was full and rich and round and flat all at once. She was stunning. The kind of beauty usually reserved for models. Push stared openly at her, surprised and astonished by the way she was standing, the casual beauty of her, but the reaction of Thorsen was even more noticeable.

He stood transfixed, openly ogling her—breathing in long pulls, his eyes locked into her's, his one hand raised as if to knock again, a word half finished out of his mouth. "Nnnnnngggg."

She said nothing, studied them both with a question in her eyes as she recognized the manager. Maybe Dave has found a new kind of therapy, Push thought.

CHAPTER FIVE

Push worked on one of Scarf's burritos, spooned more green chilis over the top of it in a steaming heap of liquid fire, and took a huge forkful. The lean ground meat, very few beans, some lettuce and tomato and Scarf's secret ingredient—a measure of instant mashed potatoes mixed with the meat—somehow combined with the chili sauce to give the concoction more body, depth. Then Push backed a small truck of green chili sauce up to the plate and dumped it, seeds and all, over the top of the burrito. Two bites made sweat break out on the forehead and upper lip and by the third bite speech was impossible.

He ate the burrito in silence, ignoring the rest of the people at the bar. It was nearly midnight and he was in that stage of exhaustion where things seemed dreamlike. The fork moved slowly to his mouth, carried the burrito in slow motion to his tongue and he chewed abstractedly, tasting but not tasting, swallowing but not swallowing—there but not there. What he wanted, needed, was Rosa.

When he'd met her in the airport parking lot and asked her to go for a drink she'd done it—after all, how dangerous can cops be? They talked that night, and laughed some, and wound up in a motel room in a kind of grand discovery of each other's bodies, satisfying a roaring want that surprised them both. But it was more now. Now he needed it and did not understand how that had happened. He needed to make love to Rosa, then sleep next to her, feeling her move with her breath and knowing that she was there when he awakened in the night sweats. But Rosa's husband was home for a three day layover and she couldn't get away.

The husband, he thought, fog taking his brain—an enemy he didn't know, hadn't seen, had no knowledge of except for one or two comments by Rosa. And yet the man was warping his life. I want, no, I need this thing and a man I don't know is keeping me from getting it. Life. It cuts and cuts . . . he stopped the thinking. Rolling, tired thinking.

Push finished the burrito and drank the rest of the Dos Equis dark beer without putting the bottle down. He belched and Scarf took it as a signal to bring him another beer. Push nodded, drank it more slowly, paid his bill and stared out the window at Colfax. You could see the exhaust of cars streaming past. A thick gas that mixed with the hot summer night and gave body to the air and heat and noise. Everybody and nobody going everywhere and no place. Jesus, he thought, I'm getting heavy. Two beers and a burrito and I'm getting heavy.

It had been an upside down frustrating day. Of

course most of them were. Far and away the majority of time in any investigation was finding out information that went nowhere. And this case was going that way. Kate had known nothing—or at least nothing Push had found out. Thorsen had given him the high sign and Push had left to question other tenants who might know where Betti could be, leaving Thorsen alone with Kate.

Therapy.

Thorsen was with her now, or was earlier. He had asked her to dinner and she had accepted. Just like that. Thorsen was good looking, in a boyish way, and there was also the cop thing. Push had seen it before, especially with Thorsen. Something about policemen was attractive to certain women. Perhaps that they were safe, secure. Or at least appeared to be. Safe. Christ. He wondered if Thorsen had told her he was married yet.

No. Not yet.

The rest of the afternoon they had done legwork. They checked with Transair—Betti's employer—but were unable to find out anything about her whereabouts. Her supervisor was angry because Betti hadn't called in but became worried and helpful when she realized that Betti might be in some kind of trouble. She was a tall, thin woman who had been a stewardess. Push enjoyed watching her. It was as if she knew exactly where her hands and feet were going to be long before they went there, Push thought, watching her move around her office at Stapleton Airport as she answered their questions. Everything just so.

"Betti has on only one other occasion not shown up

for work and not been able to call. She was caught up in Evergreen last October and it snowed over thirty inches. The telephone lines went out as well as the roads and she didn't get down or get word to us for two days." The supervisor consulted a file. Push noted that her nails were chewed. Everything wasn't that smooth with her then. It must be a hard job running all those attendants. Rosa chewed her nails. He shook his head.

"How long has she worked here?"

Another look at the file. "Six years. Plus a month. Never late, only one absence—the one I told you about."

"Had she been married?"

The supervisor hesitated. "I think we're getting into an area that might be a bit personal. I mean if she comes back tomorrow I'm not sure she would be happy about her personal life becoming public."

Thorsen had been sitting in silence in a chair next to the desk. He now coughed and raised his head. "It's not like it will be public—we're police officers. We keep everything in confidence." A bald lie, that, but Push said nothing. Police kept almost nothing in confidence. "We're investigating a possible murder here . . ."

"I understand. But why do you think it might be Betti?"

Push cut in. "Somebody called her in as missing. If you were worried enough to call her in as missing why are you so worried now about telling us about her?"

She closed the file. "There must be some mistake—I didn't call her in missing."

Push studied her. "Somebody called her in missing. We assumed it was you."

She shook her head. "I didn't, nor to my knowledge did anybody at Transair . . ."

And they knew it wasn't anybody at the apartment complex. Push rubbed his face, thinking. Somebody called her in missing. Who? A friend? The killer? Why? But hell, if it was a true cutter there didn't have to be any sense to it. Son of a bitch probably thought he was helping her somehow. Or wanted them to know about it. Wanted to be caught. Enough. It was all bullshit thinking.

"Does it say what blood type Betti is?" He almost said was. "We have reason to believe the victim was type B, positive."

The supervisor looked once more at the file and Push could see the color leave her face. "Type B—positive. My god."

"Was or had she been married?" Thorsen asked again.

The supervisor nodded slowly. "Yes. She was married to a man named Jerry Brickner. They got a divorce two, no, two and a half years ago. So many of them break up. It's the travel you know. If they stay working and married something has to suffer. The travel causes trouble."

"I don't suppose there is an address for Brickner in the file, is there?"

There hadn't been, but they found Brickner by going through the motor vehicle department. He was home with his new wife when they went to interview him. He looked to Push like a model of a man, a robot. Hair combed just a certain way, trim body, well-muscled—a model man. Almost plastic skin, stretched over a six foot plastic frame, living in a plastic house with a plastic life. He looks, Push thought when they met him, like he was designed to be married to a stewardess. He was cooperative, friendly, hadn't seen Betti in several weeks, when they'd met once for lunch to talk over some papers about some property they owned jointly but were selling, and was there anything else he could do, thank you?

His eyes had looked hinky. There was something there, and they both felt it. He was too helpful, too much of everything. Push could smell it. But then everyone was looking hinky to him these days. "Where were you about a week ago?"

He was in the construction business and had been working on a house out in Lakewood, coming home at night, going to work in the morning except for a couple of nights when he had to work late. All the time he was talking, Push kept thinking of those war books above the bed and he made a mental note to call on Brickner later, when the new wife wasn't around. But they didn't have to, because as they left, he came out and stopped them before they got to the car. He kept looking over his shoulder at the house.

"I wasn't being exactly honest," he told them. The truth was he'd been seeing his ex—been visiting now and then with Betti. They couldn't be married—fought all the time—but they still enjoyed being in bed together and he didn't want his present wife to know about it. But he had a date with Betti and she hadn't showed and when he'd called Transair she wasn't there and he'd been the one who called in the anonymous missing report on her. It wasn't like her to just not be somewhere that way.

"Only . . . can you keep my name out of it?" he'd asked. "My new wife will kill me if she thinks I've been seeing Betti . . ."

It had been late evening when they got done with Brickner.

Quinsey had wanted to see them but they dragged ass getting back to headquarters and he was gone for the day. It was something they were good at, avoiding Quinsey. It was something everybody in the detective division was good at, avoiding Quinsey.

A frustrating day.

And when he called Rosa she'd told him her husband's flight was canceled and he was on the layover and that left him alone.

Frustrating.

He hated being alone at night. It wasn't sex. It was the aloneness. He was tired beyond sleep and there would be no rest in his apartment, save to lie awake and hope his body relaxed because it was prone. He had done much of that, mostly just after the divorce. The messy little divorce. The man whose car he had trashed—he smiled at the pun, thinking of it—had moved in with his ex before he was really out of the apartment, and that had torn at Push like a claw. Twice he had gone by to beat the shit out of the man, or probably kill him, but something had stopped him and he hadn't gone in. After that he would just go by, usually drunk, usually without knowing quite why—often just to sit and watch. He thought at first he missed her but he didn't—not really. It was the other thing. He didn't want to be alone. Not then, not later, after the divorce, and not now.

He thought of getting a room at some cheap motel— there were motels up and down Colfax where they wouldn't charge him except for sheets, places they called cop drops where all the men took what they called their seconds. And he had used them several times, although never for Rosa. Never a cheap motel or cop drop for Rosa, although once they had done it on a back road near Evergreen in the rear seat of his unmarked police car.

But he hated going to those places alone and now that he was with Rosa, at least when her husband was out of town, he did not want to call one of the other women he knew and had spent time with and he did not want to use hookers, although he had done that on more than one occasion.

Frustrating.

The other cops at Scarf's were starting to get drunk and mean and it was time to leave. The car was a Dodge and had vapor-locked in the heat and took a bit to start. It was still hot, midnight-hot on Colfax, midnight-neon-hot and he drove with the windows down, letting his stink blow off. The motor sounded all right when he kicked it a couple of times so it must be cooler than it was during the day, though it didn't feel that way. The air coming in the window seemed hot and flat, smokey with exhaust.

He couldn't bring himself to go back to his apartment. Sit there and stare at a tube, drink beer until he went numb, close his eyes, wait for sleep and it wouldn't come. Shit.

I might as well work, he thought, accelerating. Midnight on a Friday night and I might as well work. What the hell, Thorsen isn't home—he's with his new therapy. He's working. Sort of.

There could be something on the street. There's always something on the street. Could be something about the cutter. He slowed down, watching the sidewalks. It didn't start coming alive until after midnight. Some cops thought that when AIDS came—they called it the Gay Gasher and the Fag Fucker—it would slow things down on the street. It hadn't had the slightest noticeable effect except that some, not all, but some of the gays were a bit more cautious.

The beers, or the beers mixed with the exhaustion, had him feeling slightly fuzzy. He shook his head to clear it, thought of where to start.

Petey's. The slime bar. Petey's was a good place to start. It was nearby, four more blocks, and he cruised easily. There were hookers working. Summer hookers. Short shorts, tight tank tops, with lots of breast showing. He saw two of them working some john in a pickup with a gun rack and they waved when he went by. He knew them both from vice but they knew he worked homicide now. It made him a safe cop and there wasn't anything safer than a safe cop. He thought about stopping to talk to them but they were working and it would blow the john away if he stopped. If it was a slow night he might be the only john they got, or one of two or three. If he stopped it might kill their whole night's income.

He'd hit Petey's and then come back and talk to the hookers when they got done with the john.

Unlike some seedy bars that started as decent places and went downhill, Petey's had never been what could be termed a "nice" bar. Built during the fifties with two phoney arches and covered in pink stucco that must have immediately begun to fall off in patches, showing the chicken wire underneath, it seemed to have been designed for sleaze—a place for off-duty hookers, drug freaks, pushers, what Thorsen called the people with sores on their faces. There was a pink neon sign that said PETEY across the stucco on the street side and somehow it had never burned out, although nobody could ever remember anybody named Petey who had owned the joint or worked there. A gravel space full of potholes provided what passed for a parking lot and Push bounced in and parked. It felt like the shocks were going as well. The maintenance department never did anything with the cars except check the oil.

He hesitated before opening the door, checked the parking lot. Two pickups, both with gun racks—he hated pickups with gun racks, hated people other than cops having guns—and three cars. Plus the streetwalkers. Not so many. He disliked going into crowded bars. Booze talked hard and made people crazy and if there were many of them you couldn't watch them all.

The door was glass painted black, heavy and prone to stick. He put his shoulder against it and pushed it in. Inside, the bar ran straight away from the door. It was totally dark except for the light that came from the canoe scene lamp over the bar on one side and a bare light bulb over the pool table at the back.

At the bar were three men and four women—sitting there to drink. Shooting pool were two cowboy types. In a booth were two men, skinny, with guts from beer and edema. The place smelled of piss and stale beer. The bartender was a stout man, wearing a tee shirt so dirty that the saying on it was impossible to read. His name was Clayton and when he saw Push walk in he put a can of Coors on the bar. Push hated Coors, but hated it less than everything else in the bar—they didn't have any dark beer. They didn't have anything except Old Milwaukee and Coors and a back bar full of bottles of hard liquor that hadn't been opened in years. Petey's didn't draw people who drank hard liquor. Didn't draw any class drinkers. Didn't draw yuppies. Not even if they were cruising.

Push took a sip of the beer, did not put any money on the bar. It wasn't expected. Clayton had worked at Petey's long enough to know all the cops, know all the things about all the cops that came in. Cops didn't pay. If you were lucky, cops didn't take. Push had tried to pay once, long ago, but Clayton had shoved the money onto the floor and that was the end of it. He nodded to Push, leaned over the bar.

"What do you need?"

Push smiled. "You don't think I'd come in here for just a drink, pass the time of night?"

"Shit. You want that you go to Scarf's. You come here when you need something or want to catch a disease. What's shaking?" Clayton had done time once for assault but Push knew about the case and it had been a bad rap. There had been many times when Clayton could have done time on good raps and hadn't gotten caught, but the time he went to Canyon City had been a bad one. They almost but not quite liked each other, the way many cops seemed to like cons more than normal people. They had more in common. If Push thought about it, he was closer to Clayton and this bar than he was to Matherson. If he thought about it. He didn't. Subconsciously, instinctively he knew he wasn't close to either. He was a cop.

"I need to know if there's anything new on the street."

"New? Hell, man, there's never anything new on the street. New in what way?"

"I work homicide."

"So you mean new in a death way?"

Push nodded.

Clayton looked up and down the bar, thinking. Petey's was owned by three stockbrokers who had bought the place for the property under it and then found that they could write off the loss each year, juggle some money through the bar and come out with a very smooth profit. They kept only the loosest of possible tabs on Clayton, who hit the till like Atilla the Hun hitting Asia, and Clayton in turn was very conscious of his customers—those who spent the money he raided. He did not consider them human, quite. And he was relatively certain at least some of them had committed one or another form of assault and that probably at least some of them had killed somebody. It was that kind of bar. If he got a reputation as a snitch the regulars would move on to some other sleaze bar on Colfax—there were many—and he would be out his income.

On the other hand he knew Push to be fair and relatively honest. And Push could do him trouble. Cops could always do somebody trouble.

"I tell you, Push, could you be a little more exact on that?" He wiped his hands on his tee shirt and leaned to whisper. "I mean you know my customers, right? Any given night you could find most any kind of crime you want in here . . ."

Push looked at the bar again. At the far end a man and a woman sat—he thought he knew the woman but couldn't be sure. She was thin but had nice breasts under a pullover, just starting to get drunk, eyes closing a little slowly. Damn, where did he know her from? Thin face, good lips, round, brown eyes. Sally. No, Sarah something. Used to be married to a trucker who beat her. Yeah. "Is there any word on the street about somebody going whacko?"

Clayton waited. Shrugged. "Hell, we're all whacko . . ."

"I mean threatening to cut hookers up, anything like that." Yeah, Sarah something. Couldn't remember the last name. She looked up and caught him staring, smiled.

Even teeth. Not pretty but not ugly. He thought of Rosa and missed her, could not think of being alone, could not imagine another night of being alone, the reaching, empty loneliness of it—he hated it. He smiled back at the woman. She remembered him, slid easily off the stool and came to him, walking slowly, moving her hips in a gentle roll.

Clayton leaned back. "I haven't heard nothing about that kind of thing but if I do I'll call you."

"You do that." He turned to the woman. "Hello."

"You're a cop," she said, flatly. "We met at a party, two, three years ago."

"I thought I knew you. It's Sarah, isn't it?"

She nodded. "I came into the john at the party and you were throwing up in the bathtub."

"I always try to make a good impression."

"You said it reminded you of your ex-wife."

"Not all of her." Push smiled. "Just part. Part of her looks like a bathtub. Can I buy you a beer or are you with somebody?"

"I'm with you." She ignored the man at the bar who was watching them and the man made no move to get off his stool. "Let's go."

"Just what I like—a shy woman." Push moved aside to let her go out the door first.

"We'll go to my place," she said over her shoulder, "but you have to promise not to throw up in my bathtub."

Interiors
One

They could never understand him.

And he was not vague about it. He knew exactly who "they" were—they were the spectators. The people who had nothing to do with life as it counted but merely went along with it, moved with the flow the way fish moved with a river, never understanding why they moved or where they were going to be next. Those who only watched. Other people did not understand it—life. And they could never understand him.

Red was part of it. The glow around his mother's head was red and blood was red and until they could know the importance of blood they would not understand life. Without blood there could be no life, could be no hope for the rest of them. Without blood there could be no spirit, no tie with the gods, with the ancient ones.

Blood was in all, but in the chosen ones the blood and the bodies were sacred; were given to sacrifice for the spirit of life, to insure the happiness and fullness of the gods.

It was not a question of good or evil, right or wrong. That's what "they" would never understand. There were things that were and things that weren't; a way things had to be and it surprised him that many of the chosen did not understand. They should know, should feel the joy of it.

The last one had not understood any part of it, even when he explained it to her on the mountain road in the headlights. He had told her the whole story there while she stupidly cried and begged; told her how he was chosen, how he had been in Mexico and found the secret in the pyramids of the Aztecs, in the stones that had run with blood; told her how the chosen ones then had longed for it, longed to meet the knife, but she had heard none of it.

She had gotten out of hand, hysterically jerking at the ropes until they made marks on her and almost ruined her so that she would not have been acceptable. And he had worked so hard to tell her all the facets of it—that it wouldn't be bad, that he had precise instructions on how it was to be done so there would be no pain and on how to notify the others when it was done by sending chosen parts to the far places. You are wonderful, he'd told her, chosen by the gods for your beauty, given the glow around your head for the beauty of your soul, but she had heard none of it.

She had mistaken all of it and thought he wanted only the other thing when that wasn't even part of why he was doing it—wasn't any part of it. He did the other thing all the time. Even with his wife. It surprised him when she had thought that it was all about sex. It wasn't anything to do with sex.

He was, as always, thankful that he had been given the ability to see those who were chosen. Of course the chosen were all women, they had that much in common—that's because they alone were special ones. Men were not suitable because they lacked the grace and beauty the gods wanted. Women were the containers for the gods; they were the primary carriers and they were the only ones who could have the aura.

It was all so ancient and perfect. Everything had been worked out by the Aztecs and he marveled at times on the luck of it. Had he not gone to Mexico on a vacation, had he not gone to the Aztec temples and the museums he would not have heard the voices; would not have known he was to be selected by the ancient gods to be one of them.

The ones who were to be chosen started to come to him soon after his trip to Mexico. At first he did not know what to do with them and he botched two of them by just killing them and leaving the bodies. He did not at first understand the ritual, the core of the ritual that made them correct for the gods. Then it came to him, in the place between sleep and dreaming one night where things can be real and unreal it came to him how to do them correctly; how they must be distributed to give full notice for the gods.

After that they came to him rapidly, sometimes so fast he could not take them all. He didn't have to hunt them or go to find them. They came to him with a special light over them, a light around their head and shoulders that only he could see—the same red glow his mother had around her head when he was a boy, the glow from the gods to show they were chosen as his mother had been chosen.

The Aztecs knew. With their great temples and blood rituals, the pyramids and sacrifices, they had known all along. He'd read everything he could find about them. They were experts at the ritual and they had been limited to Stone Age technology, had been forced to literally use stone knives, no drugs—really limited. But they knew, knew what was going on.

Sometimes it amazed him. When he worked and sat for such long periods and had nothing to do but think it amazed him how few people truly understood the Aztecs or the whole concept of blood, the chosen glow of red that made them ready for the ritual.

Sometimes he felt terribly alone and thought he might be the only one. But then he would see the glow on the next chosen one and the feeling would leave. It was just that the ancient ones had not told him but of course they had their own reasons for silence and he did not question it.

It was enough that he had been given the ritual to perform. He did not need to know more.

CHAPTER
SIX

Push opened his eyes slowly, tried to remember where he was, put the night together.

Oh, yeah, Petey's. And Sarah. He had driven Sarah home. Yeah.

The ceiling was textured with glitter and there was daylight coming around a shade catching the little shiny pieces, making them look like cheap stars. The room was cooled by a whirring air conditioner in the window and he thought for a moment it could be any time or any day. A darkened strange bedroom in a darkened strange place in any day and any time and he felt strangely relaxed, loose.

He was completely naked. Not even a watch. From some other room there was sound, dishes being moved, scraping, a woman humming—a country and western tune—and the smell of cooking. Peppers, some peppers were frying with something else. Garlic and grease.

He looked around the bedroom. His clothes were over a chair near the foot of the bed and he could see the butt of his gun still in the holster. On a table next to the bed he found his watch and a pack of Winstons. She must smoke. Funny, he smiled, she didn't taste like she smoked.

They had vodka and he must have nearly passed out. He remembered making love once—she screamed and clawed when she came—and they must have done it again but he didn't remember it except that he felt limp still, and weak. As if he'd been sick but was moving towards recovery. There was a hangover kicking at the base of his neck but it was mild, almost gentle.

He clawed the watch over. Ten-thirty. Late. Dave would be wondering what in hell happened. Or maybe not. Dave might be late as well, if his therapy worked out all right. He might not even be up yet.

"Good morning." The door opened and Sarah came in. She was naked and somehow her tousled hair made her thinness look voluptuous. Her breasts hung slightly, swayed with her walk. "I thought I heard movement."

"I smell something cooking."

"Breakfast. I started the sauce for chilireanoes but that's for later. I'm not done with you yet."

She slid into bed and pushed him down, used her mouth on him until he was ready, and then sat on him, moving slowly until he thought his temples would explode. Finally, screaming and thrashing, she climaxed and fell next to him, lay quietly.

"Good morning." He said at last, gasping for air. "You have a strange way to get people up."

"I'm working on it . . ."

"I won't be able to move for a week."

"I could live with that."

He closed his eyes and meant for it to be only for a second. Meant to open them again and call Dave, but sleep took him, clean and down and away, and when he next opened his eyes he saw that it was close to noon. She was standing next to the bed, fully clothed. She was wearing a smart, business-type dress, and holding a plate full of eggs and chilis.

"I have to go to work. Here is a plate of something to fill you up and bring you back to life." She hesitated. "If you wanted to stay I wouldn't mind."

"I'll have to leave. Work. You know."

She nodded. "I thought that. Lock the door behind you when you leave." She put the plate on the table next to the bed.

"I'll call . . ." He started to say more but she had turned away, and in a moment he heard the front door close behind her. "Thank you."

He tried the eggs, found them to be delicious, and ate them sitting in bed. When he finished them he took the plate to the kitchen and put it in the dishwasher. He found a glass and drank three glasses of cold water and started to feel human. Then he took a quick shower, washed with some soap he found hanging on a rope that smelled like his backyard when he was a kid, some kind of flowers he couldn't name, and when he was clean and dressed picked up the phone next to the bed.

A detective named Harliss answered at the station. He was new, not a kid but new as a detective and still eager. That would be gone soon. Tall, but with a gut that showed more at the sides than the front, he spoke in a funny gasp, as if he were always trying to catch his breath. "Thorsen said you'd call. He went up to Idaho Springs and told me to tell you that you should come up there immediately. Go to the sheriff's substation up there and they'll tell you where he is. Then he said to tell you number seven. Does that mean anything?"

"No—it's just a joke between us." Push hung up and made for the door. He and Dave had worked out a simple code in case they needed to say things in front of suspects. Eight meant take over, I have to take a shit. Silly numbers. Seven meant that it was important and to drop everything else. Seven meant it was critical.

Outside the apartment building the air hit him like a hot wall. He couldn't remember where he'd parked and it took him a moment to find the car. When he opened the door it smelled like somebody had crawled inside and died of body odor.

Cop cars all smelled like stations, always smelled bad. Why is it, he thought, that crime always smelled bad?

The car started easily—which surprised him—and he rolled the windows down and in ten minutes was moving well on I-70 heading west up into the mountains, sucking the hot wind and smog into his lungs, hoping it would be cool in the mountains.

Idaho Springs was an old mining town more or less huddled in a valley along I-70 as it climbed the mountains and headed west. Like so many other old mining towns, it had been taken over by the people from the city and was now geared to tourism although some small mines remained.

Law in all those small towns came from the Jefferson County Sheriff in Golden, Colorado, but each town had a sheriff substation and that was what Dave had meant.

Push drove easily, kept it at seventy, and was heartened to feel the air become cool and clean-smelling as he started climbing past Lookout Mountain into Genesee Pass. When he reached the top of the pass the temperature was almost too cool with the windows open and he saw that the peaks spread out before him were covered with snow though it was late June. After all the years in Colorado, Push was still startled by how rapidly the weather could change. You could drive an hour west of Denver and be in a completely different world.

He let the car follow the freeway down in the gentle curving loops from Genesee Pass, past the El Rancho restaurant and the turnoff for Evergreen—he thought of Rosa and had a moment of guilt for the night with Sarah but they had agreed to no strings, other than her husband, of course, and he was a hell of a string. Then why guilt? Maybe Push felt guilty for Sarah's sake. He turned the thinking off as the freeway wound further into the mountains.

In twenty more minutes he saw Idaho Springs. The sheriff's substation was near the exit from the freeway and he walked into the small building to find it manned by a deputy who happened to be a young woman. She was pretty with tightly cut short hair and wide brown eyes and was small, so small he would not have thought they would have hired her, but her uniform fit well and she seemed tightly muscled. Her size made the magnum on her belt look like a cannon. The full grips seemed to cover half her waist.

Push identified himself. "I was told to come here—what's up?"

"A body—all cut to hell. Some hikers found it and when we called it in they said it might tie in with something you guys are working on. Your partner is already up there, been there an hour. I'll take you up."

"Up" proved to be winding back up into a series of old mining roads that led into the mountains above Idaho Springs with grades so steep and cutbacks so tight that a regular car could never have done it. The deputy—her name was Judy—drove the department Bronco efficiently, swearing expertly on the turns while Push held his breath and looked down over hundred-foot drops into rockpiles. Twice the Bronco jerked sideways when the tires slipped on moving rocks, and each time he thought they were going to go over but Judy kept driving as if it were normal and he forced his buttock muscles to loosen up.

"Nice road," he said once but she either didn't hear him over the whine of the engine or chose to ignore him. He thought the latter and turned back to watching the view as the Bronco climbed back and forth.

Well above Idaho Springs—the buildings looked like toys—the trail suddenly turned back through a cut and came out in a small canyon, really nothing more than a large gully. At the end of the gully was an old tin shed, the tin rusted and mostly caved in, and in front of the shed were three more Broncos and half a dozen men standing over something on the ground. He recognized Dave's tall form at once, as Dave angled over to speak to one of the men in uniform. Two younger people stood by one of the Broncos. There were backpacks resting on the ground next to them and he guessed that would be the hikers. Brilliant deduction he thought—the detective's mind at work.

Push jumped out of the Bronco ahead of Judy and walked to Dave before looking at the body—as it proved to be—on the ground.

"Did you get home?"

Dave shook his head. "I was with you. We worked all night."

Push nodded. "Right. What's with the body?"

"Ten to one it's her," Dave said. "But she's so fucked up it's going to be hard to prove it." A man standing next to him held out his hand and Dave introduced him. "This is Sheriff Carson. Technically he's in charge but he's turned it over to us. I told him about the breasts we've found."

Push nodded and shook hands, then moved past the two men to view the body. Judy came up about then and she apparently had not seen it because she took a quick look, like a kid peeking, then turned away. She didn't throw up but he could hear her fighting it. "Breathe deep on the sides of your tongue," he told her, as he'd been told by Packard. "Sometimes it helps . . ."

The thing on the ground couldn't truly be called a body. The head was gone, both hands were gone—not just cut off but gone—and the legs had been removed from the torso, cut where the hips joined the tops of the legs, at the joint, but were still in position as if the killer had tried to put them back on. Both breasts were also removed but the body had not been eviscerated and the vagina had not been mutilated. Strange, that—usually anything sexual was taken, or at least cut. The Boston Strangler had left things in the old ladies he killed, broom handles, kitchen utensils, bottles. All of them seemed to do sexual things. Unless they were into ritualistic work. Maybe that was it. A group. Not one man or woman but a group. Like back in the livestock mutilation days. Satanist cults.

The stomach looked young. Flat and clean, except for the inevitable blood smears, and young as he supposed the stomach of Betti Fencer would have looked when she was alive. Moving up and down the aisles of an airplane, taking trays, bringing them, smiling. How can you smile now Betti, without a head?

He turned back to Dave. "Have you started any searching?"

"I was just starting it now. I haven't been here very long. It took forever to get up here."

"We might find the other parts of the body," Push spoke to the deputies, little more than kids, really, and probably not trained that well in evidence procedures "But we're going after any other evidence as well. Body parts aren't going to help us as much as something about

GARY PAULSEN

the asshole who did this—a cigarette butt, a hair, boot
and tire marks. We need it all. Move carefully and look at
every inch."

Push had the deputies spread out and he went back
to the body. No coincidences, he thought, so this must be
her. If that was a given then she might have been here a
week, yet there was little evidence of decomposition. The
corpse looked a bit old, gray, but no real rot had set in and
it looked fresher than the breasts had looked. There was
blood smell but not the stink of rot.

Temperature. Both breasts were in airports, warm
places. The body had been up here in the mountains
where it was cool. That could be it, must be it.

He examined the wounds closely. They were relatively clean and even. The neck looked almost surgically
removed. What had the pathologist said? Oh, yes, a long
very sharp knife pulled back and forth in a sawing motion.
He saw similar cut lines on the torso where the breasts
had been removed, the long ridges made by the same
motion.

The ground was rocky and he couldn't see any footprints of any kind. But there were skid marks, blood
rubbed on the rock as if the torso had been dragged to
where it lay. He stood and followed the skid marks with
his eyes, saw that they led to a wider dark area near a rock
outcropping that formed a low wall leading back into the
mountain. He walked to the patch on the ground and saw
that the darkness had been caused by blood soaking into
the rocks and dirt. That would explain the lack of blood
where the torso lay now.

Judy had tried to look again and was now being ill in back of the Bronco. Jesus, he thought, I was that way once. Now I could probably eat a goddam sandwich.

He went back once more to the torso. Dave must have called for the body people to come up from Denver and usually they would wait to move the body until then. But he didn't feel like waiting and he used one toe to raise the torso and look underneath it. There were no cuts on the back and nothing on the ground. He let it back easily, then returned to the darkened place on the ground.

There was some dirt there, which must have eroded from the rock face above, and in the thin layer of soil he saw one footprint. It was an intricate pattern, the kind on popular running shoes. Too large to have been made by a woman. A man, size ten maybe, or ten and a half.

Is it you? Is this where you stood, you son of a bitch? He shook his head. Hell, it could be anybody, could be one of the deputies. He had to quit that kind of jump in logic. That never worked.

"Over here!" A deputy yelled, almost happily. "I found the head!"

Push followed the sound of the voice to the back of the tin shed where he found a sheriff's deputy standing in front of a pile of small chipped rocks. Apparently the shed had contained a rock crusher of some kind and it had spewed the waste out the back to dump it in a pile. This slag heap was fifteen feet high and perhaps forty feet across at the base. In the side a kind of depression had been scooped out at eye level and the head had been set back into the hole, facing out. Tousled brown-red hair matted with blood. The eyes were open, but glazed and without expression, and the mouth was also partially open in a macabre smile. It was her, Betti. He recognized her from the picture clipped to her employment form. Hello, he thought with a deep sadness—hello Betti.

On both sides were the cut-off hands, lying palm down but in close as if to help hold the head up.

"It's her," Dave said after another minute of silence. "It's like some kind of goddam altar."

Push still said nothing but he had exactly the same thought. It looked like some religious altar the way the head was set back into the rock pile, facing out with the hands to either side. That might explain why the vagina hadn't been mutilated. It was some cult thing, some religious bullshit.

Then he saw them. In the sand by the side of the shed, he saw two footprints with the same intricate pattern as the one he'd seen by the bloodstain. He'd stood right here then, right next to them, stood and looked at the head right next to where Dave and Push now stood.

Push took a deep breath and turned away. He felt sad and sick, and deeply tired even though he had slept a good solid night with Sarah.

"This sucks . . ." Dave sighed. "I was going to go home tonight. I think maybe I'm over that other thing and I was going to go home and see if it's all right. Now . . . it just sucks."

"So what the hell," Push said, heading back for the Bronco to make sure the body wagon was coming. "When doesn't it suck?"

CHAPTER
SEVEN

Driving past his ex-wife's house was as instinctive to him now as breathing, but her Camaro was gone so he didn't slow down and look at the building as he would have if her car had been there.

It was stupid. He knew that. She was married and it was done and finished and he hadn't spoken to her in over a year and had no idea what she was doing with herself and yet he drove past her apartment building. He couldn't help it.

At first, just after the separation, it had been worse. Then he had got drunk every night, not just high but stinking, puking, piss-your-pants drunk and he would drive to her apartment house and sit until he passed out, waiting. Just waiting. He never spoke to her, saw her only two or three times, but four or five nights a week he would park there, so drunk he had to close one eye while driving, so drunk he was stopped many times by patrolmen who made him drink coffee before releasing him to drive on and stop, stop and wait.

Stupid.

Now he did it automatically. Didn't go to sit there and wait but drove past, as he did so, and thought—when he thought of it at all—that perhaps in another year he might not even drive by any longer. God knew he didn't want her, didn't want to see her or speak to her, would not be involved again with her under any circumstances and he figured in a year, maybe less, he'd get out of the habit.

But he drove past now, on his way from the station to Scarf's for a beer and burrito. I am, he thought, certifiably whacked-out. Divorce-whacked-out. He knew one cop who, after his divorce, could not face the day unless he put his left sock on first each morning. Push had thought that was strange and now . . . now it didn't seem so strange. Jesus, he thought, we're some group. Dave can't

get it up, I can't give it up, and I have the balls to laugh at a guy for putting a sock on.

The medical examiner had been jovial when he got the body.

"Yup—that's the one who had the tits. I'll check blood type but I can tell from the cuts it must be the same one." He had assembled the body on the metal table so that it was more or less back together, the head and legs and hands in the right place, though disconnected. "I'll get enough blood now to make some solid tests. We found traces of drugs in the breasts but there wasn't enough to get a good reaction . . ."

"What kind of drugs?"

"Valium."

"No. The liquid. My guess is she'd been injected with liquid Valium, a pretty fair load, before he started cutting. She might even have had enough to kill her so that she was unconscious or going into a coma when he started. Although her heart was beating when he cut off her breasts. But from our initial findings it looked like a massive shot or it wouldn't have shown up as strong as it did in the breast tissue. Now I can get a better indication." He had looked almost gleefully down at the body. "Also we can see what she'd been eating, drinking." And he had then taken a scalpel and cut the body from sternum down to pubis in the sweeping, radical incision of the autopsy, opening the crude cut left by the killer.

"I'll call," he said to Push's back as Push turned and walked away. "Probably tomorrow or the next day when the test results get back. Goddam lab is getting slower every day . . ."

They had worked all day in Idaho Springs, then returned to the station, and except for two footprints and a solid ID on the body they had come up empty. Tomorrow they would start doing nuts and bolts, talking to all her friends, working again on the ex-husband, digging. But now there was nothing. At nine o'clock Dave said to hell with it and went home to ". . . try out my tool," leaving Push in the station to greet the night shift.

Technically there were no homicide detectives working the night shift. Homicide was usually a day job only. But everything seemed to happen at night, and much of the information that came to the police seemed to filter through the dark. So many cases were solved with luck, bits that came together out of nowhere. For that reason, Push liked to brief the night people, when he was working on a hot case, even if they were working burglary, just in case they ran into something that might help.

He sat at his desk. Most of the men had gone home or were out working and the only other person in the squad room was a burglary detective named Cartier. Cartier was an old hand and completely addicted to gambling. It was said that he owed not only every bookie in Denver but would owe their grandchildren as well. The only reason they let him keep gambling was that they were afraid to turn him off because he was a cop and would start busting them. As it was they were safe and he bet on everything, anything. Once he bet on a scene in a movie while sitting in a theater, bet on which way the actor would move next. He worked just for the bookies and yet was an excellent burglary cop. He made good, solid arrests and held the department record for returned goods. His record looked good on annual reports and made his superiors look good; for that reason they left him alone about his gambling.

Cartier was sitting at the other end of the room at a desk reading a racing form. When he saw he was alone with Push he threw the form down and walked slowly to the desk next to him, sat and put his feet up on the desk.

"How's your life?"

Push had been staring down at the desk, thinking of Rosa, thinking he would call her. A small corner of his mind also kept thinking of Sarah and the looseness, the relaxed way she had left him, but he knew it would probably not help. Not just getting laid. Another lonely night was coming and the sadness was cornering him and he thought it might have something to do with Betti Fencer. Seeing her that way. It wasn't that bad—not as bad as many cases he'd seen—but something about the waste of it made him melancholy and he couldn't shake it.

And now Cartier was sitting there, talking to him. Cartier hadn't spoken to Push in six months. Why now?

"I'm sliding by," Push said. "Day to day—how about you?"

Cartier shrugged. "Could be better."

"You winning?"

"Shit."

Push leaned back, looked at the ceiling. It was made of drop-in tiles and there were stains from a leak. What made that strange is there were three floors above and he wondered what kind of a leak would come down four floors. What in hell did Cartier want? Push was determined not to ask.

"You used to work with Packard, didn't you?"

Push kept looking at the ceiling. "Yes. Years ago."

Cartier sighed. "Man, those were the days. A cop like Packard, he could get things done . . ."

Ahh, Push thought—here it comes.

"How long did you work with him?"

Push shrugged. "Two, three years."

"You get pretty solid?"

Push turned to him. "Look, Cartier, let's cut the crap. Where is all this going?"

Cartier studied him. He was a thin man but not a healthy, tall thin like Thorsen. More a pale thin. Snake thin. Gambling was harder on a man than drinking or drugs. "I need to get something done. They say you've still got the machinery to get things done—Packard's machinery."

"Who says that?"

Cartier looked away, then back. "You know, around. They say you helped on that Malley business . . ."

Packard's legacy. The feudal police state. The fact was the law more often than not didn't get the job done. There were too many goddam lawyers with their goddam hands out and the end result was that seldom did the law do the job it was supposed to do, either good or bad. Criminals almost always got off or wrong men got hung, depending on money and lawyers and court fights, and having nothing to do with the reality of the situation.

Packard had what he called "system cutouts." By the time the cancer took him he controlled an enormous empire in Denver. It was not an empire devoted to corruption—although Denver had been in trouble along those lines as well—so much as to societal control, power. Raw power. Packard could have been rich, immensely rich, but scorned the money. It was more a matter of control, power and control.

"Used to be a beat cop was like god," he said to Push on more than one occasion. "You ran the beat like you was god."

And he made Denver, all of Denver, his beat. If you had a kid in trouble for some minor problem you could call Packard and if he thought the kid was all right he could make a few calls and it would be settled. If somebody got away with something they shouldn't have and it looked like they were going to skate you could call Packard and Packard would have lunch with somebody and the guy would take hard time all the way down in Canyon City.

"Malley did it to himself," Push said after a moment

"Yeah, but the word is you took care of it."

Packard had come to like Push, though Push didn't care much for the older cop's views or methods, and he more or less pulled Push into his way of life. It wasn't that Push was unwilling so much as indifferent. He would be with Packard when the old beat cop was handling a problem, using his "system cutout" to avoid taking the difficulty to court, and the people involved took his presence to mean that Push was now a part of it.

Soon they began to think of Push as the next in line and when Packard lost to cancer, to smoking, to drinking, to living, Push would get the calls that Packard used to get, and he tried to stay well out of it and turned people down. He was still a virgin then and wanted to just pull his paycheck and go home, have a kid, do it all—just be a fair-play Freddy and to hell with it.

Then came Malley.

Malley was a forty-year-old Catholic priest who had developed an appetite for young boys and girls. Usually the Church handled it, moved the priest away so he could ruin a new set of children, and some priests had been "moved" ten or fifteen times for that reason. In fact in the department there was a standing rule that if an unknown molester was hitting children you checked the priests and ministers first.

But in Malley's case the priest had decided to fight it, though they had caught him committing fellatio on a ten-year-old boy in the choir room of the church and found over seven hundred pictures of children in his room. The pictures were particularly damning, showing nude boys and girls tied-up, obviously uncomfortable and afraid, and graphic closeups of their pubic areas. The priest was blatantly guilty, had kept the children silent for years by telling them god would be angry with them if they spoke, but because of his position of authority he had avoided discovery until actually caught in the act.

That the system worked at all was dubious to Push but in Malley's case it broke down completely. The priest was arrested incorrectly, the pictures taken with the wrong evidence procedures and not allowed in the trial and the priest skated.

Almost clean.

The case as a felony was thrown out because the prosecutor didn't think he could make it stick and all they could do, finally, was hang a misdemeanor charge on him—contributing to the delinquency of a minor.

He was given a month and served eighteen days with time off for time already served while awaiting trial before his bail came through.

Even the newspapers were good to the priest, unaware of the extent of his molestation, but two weeks after he was released Push got a call from the father of one of the molested boys. The father was a retired Irish Catholic policeman who had served a full twenty before pulling the pin. Push knew him vaguely.

"My kid is awake all night because he's afraid god is gonna kill him," the retired cop told Push. "The fucker ruined my kid. He'll never be the same."

"Why are you telling me?" Push had asked.

"You used to be with Packard, he said you were taking over."

"Well, I'm not."

"He said you were. He said you could take care of things. I could plant the fucker but they would catch me and I'd do time. I can't see doing time for something that sleazeball priest did. Packard said you could take care of things," he repeated quietly. "I was hoping you could help me."

And after two nights he had. Two nights of thinking what the priest had done, thinking of the seven hundred pictures, which he had seen because he was in vice then; two nights of blaming the system and thinking of the boy waiting for god to kill him. Push had used Packard's "system cutout."

It was simple, really, frighteningly easy to set up. He called a man who had a child. The man owed him a heavy favor, or more correctly owed Packard the heavy favor, and he had the man accuse the priest of molesting his child. Push made sure they named a time when the priest was alone and had no alibi and it was over. It didn't even go to court. Because the priest was on probation he was immediately busted and held with massive bail and one day during exercises in the big yard somebody killed him with a sharpened piece of thick wire through his back and into his liver. The priest bled to death internally before he could be brought to help. Push had not gone for that, just wanted him taken down, but most child molesters wound up dead anyway if they went to prison—the cons called them "short-eyes" and killed them as soon as they got a chance—and Push didn't feel that bad about the outcome. The man who killed the priest was never caught, which surprised nobody, and not too many people were sorry. A month after the death of the priest Push received a note in the mail that said, simply, "Thank you."

Two more times, on smaller problems, he had done the same thing—used Packard's connections and residual power to ". . . take care of things." Once on a rapist who got off and again on a molester who had been selling pictures of children he was molesting to underground magazines. In both cases he was approached through older cops by the parents of the victims and in both cases he remained anonymous in the solution. People knew about Malley, knew he was involved but didn't know exactly how and in the other two cases they knew nothing.

And now Cartier.

The burglary cop had been silent all this time while Push studied the ceiling, thinking, remembering Packard and the goddam sandwich.

"I got this guy," Cartier said. "Son of a bitch must have two, three hundred break-and-enters and I know it's him but the law keeps getting in the way, you know what I mean?"

Push waited, said nothing.

"Lately he's getting bolder, the way they do, and he's starting to hit when people are home. Usually women alone. So we know where it's going to go. He'll get bolder and bolder and soon there'll be assault and then a rape or somebody gets killed."

"You've busted him?"

"Eighteen times. No convictions. He had some early on, and a hell of a lot of priors, but now the son of a bitch is slippery and he's got a good lawyer."

"Who is it—his lawyer?"

"Mattson."

"Oh—no wonder he gets loose."

"Yeah. He makes enough on his fenced shit to retain someone like Mattson and he skates and I wouldn't mind, you know. It's part of the game. But he's starting to get crazy now and I want him off the goddam street before he does real damage."

Push sighed. There were questions but he didn't ask them. For Cartier to come to him when he didn't even really know Push, for him to come and ask it must be serious and he—Push—was, after all of it, a cop. He could do it or not do it, talking wouldn't change it. He had a friend, Harry Swenson. He could call Harry and set something up, and help Cartier, if he wanted to, if he thought it was worth it. Just like Packard.

Night watch people started to arrive. Two men came through the door, then another one, and Push took a piece of paper out of the drawer and handed it to Cartier. "Write his name and the case numbers and I'll look at it."

Cartier smiled. "Thanks. I wouldn't ask if I didn't mean it."

"I know."

He wrote and handed the paper to Push who jammed it into his shirt pocket.

"You want a good bet on baseball?"

"I don't gamble."

"Don't start. It's a curse."

Cartier moved away tiredly and Push decided to hell with the briefing. He'd go to Scarf's and get a burrito and a dark beer and call Rosa and hope her husband was out of town. As he went down to the parking lot in the hot night air, he tried not to think of Sarah and her thrashing and he did not think of Betti Fencer at all, not even in sadness, until he was driving and found himself going past his ex-wife's apartment on the way to Scarf's. And then it was just a quick thought, a fleeting thought of how forlorn the cut-apart body had looked on the metal table

CHAPTER
EIGHT

The phone was like salt in a wound. Push reached across Rosa who was sleeping evenly, not hearing the ringing, and pulled the receiver off the nightstand onto the floor. It stopped ringing but to reach it he had to lean further across Rosa, his face on her breast, and she moaned and moved her hips without awakening.

He held the receiver to his ear. "Yes."

"It's me," Thorsen said. "When you get around to it come down to the station."

"Emergency?"

"No. The press are here. They finally picked up on the cutter and they were waiting when I got here. Quinsey's balls are on fire and he wants a status report from us so he can deal with the hounds."

"So? Tell him our status is the same old crap—we have leads and we're expecting to make an arrest soon."

"Quinsey wants to play the game and have us give him a briefing. Just like on television."

"Just like on television."

"So give it an hour or so and drop on down. Quinsey had to run out to the jail so he'll be gone a bit." The Denver county jail was well away from the center of the city, actually out of town, and it was a major trip to go out to question a prisoner.

Push hung up and rolled back. He wished for a cigarette. He had never smoked, but he had seen a film once where a man was lying next to a beautiful woman in bed smoking a cigarette and the smoke looked so good he almost wished he had picked up the habit.

He rolled out of bed, covering Rosa with a sheet and padded to the window. Bright sun. Another hot, yellow day. His watch said it was ten o'clock but time didn't make sense to him. He went into the bathroom and turned on the light. Rosa's husband had gone out on a flight at midnight and she had met Push at an all-night restaurant. She was hungry and had eaten and he had a drink and by the time they got to the room it was three in the morning.

They had made love silently, taking from each other, and when they were done it was just dawn, the sun lighting the edge around the shade. Push had fallen into a deep sleep and not thought of work or awakening until the phone blew up.

He had no toilet articles but he brushed his teeth with a corner of a towel and took a shower and felt refreshed. When he came back into the semi-darkened room he saw Rosa was awake, her eyes open, watching him move.

"Do you have to leave?" she asked.

He shook his head. "Later. I have an hour. I didn't think you heard the phone."

She studied him silently for a moment, then motioned with a finger. "Get in bed with me. I want you in me. I want to say something to you and I want you in me."

He crawled beneath the sheets, lay on his back and she straddled him. He wasn't hard but became so in her wetness and entered her. She sat still, perfectly still, and looked down at him.

"We have to stop seeing each other."

He didn't say anything. This had happened before She had broken the relationship off several times but always called him or he would call her and they would meet and it would not end.

"I mean it this time."

He still said nothing. She was richly wet and her eyes were full of him, full of loving him, and he could hear what she said but did not believe it.

"I can't stand this anymore," she started, but her hips were moving now, pulling at him, and she was having trouble speaking. "It just isn't going anywhere . . ."

She closed her eyes and in seconds began to convulse, rolling and pulling until he could stand it no longer, and he held her while he released, his head thrashing on the pillow, his hips lifting her off the bed.

They lay together afterward, numb.

"I can't believe how that happens," she whispered. "It just comes from nowhere even when I try to control it."

"Were you serious?" He pulled himself up on a pillow. "About not seeing each other?"

She waited before answering, her hand on his stomach. "Yes. Stephen . . . feels . . . somehow different. There is something bothering him. At first I thought he might be having an affair, but I'm not sure of that. Sometimes when he comes home from trips he's moody, withdrawn. It might be just that I don't feel good in bed with him and I can't fake it any longer. I think he knows something is wrong."

"So leave him. Come with me."

She sighed. "We couldn't live together. You know that."

And he did. He knew that. They could not be apart but they could not live together. He chunked along on thirty-eight grand a year and she was used to a husband who was a captain on a major airline—over a hundred thousand a year. Push lived in an apartment that would gag most people, "small enough to piss across," according to Thorsen, "and so dirty even the roaches are sick." And she lived in a house near Evergreen that cost more than he would make in twelve years. "You've got a maid," Push once said to her, "makes more than me." Which wasn't true but made a good point. It would be a massive change for her to live at Push's level.

Plus she had no intention of marrying a cop. She had said it time and again and they had chewed on all this before. He loved her, and she loved him, but it was impossible.

"It's impossible," she said now, lying next to him. "We'll have to break it off."

But her voice had no sureness to it and he knew voices, knew people from countless interrogations, and knew that she didn't mean it. She wanted him to be the one, wanted him to take responsibility and tell her it was over but he would not, could not.

He rolled once more out of bed and into the shower. He let the water slam into the back of his neck. There was a small ache there that was turning into a headache and the hot water carried it away. She came into the bathroom—he saw her moving through the shower door—and washed her face. Then she went back into the room and dressed and was putting her makeup on, using the mirror at the vanity, when he came out.

One of them had to speak. He coughed. "Do you want me not to call?"

She shook her head. "No. I couldn't stand it."

"Ahh, hell. Let's go eat something." He pulled his trousers on and dressed while she finished her makeup. "We'll have a Mexican breakfast and then I have to get to work."

She nodded in silence but he saw that she was crying, small tears down her cheeks, and he moved to her and kissed her. "I love you."

"I know that. But it's all so complicated . . . Stephen isn't a bad person. He's good to me. I'm treating him like shit."

He said nothing, waited at the door for her to gather her purse, and let her out of the room first. There wasn't really a worry but she insisted on being let out first and he would follow in a minute or so.

"Otherwise it looks so tacky," she said. "Just tromping out of the room together . . ."

He waited a moment and followed her out. The smell from their lovemaking was thick in the room and stayed in his nostrils and mind as he walked down the hall to the exit.

By the time Push got to the station, the press were already waiting in the squad room—two newspaper reporters and two different camera crews with two serious young on-camera reporters. Quinsey was back, had walked in just ahead of Push and moved to the back corner of the squad room where they normally held interviews. It was out of the way and had a "blank" background where people couldn't wave or flip the bird, which would ruin the interview—something Thorsen or Push did whenever they got a chance to be on camera.

Push hated the press. Most cops found them to be a meddling obstacle, kept tripping over reporters and were sometimes openly interfered with by them—especially in a hostage or otherwise tense situation. It was not uncommon for the press, in the person of a cameraman and anchorman or woman, to completely "take over" a case and the results were almost always disastrous. Police control of a situation was based on strength, force, firmness; for a criminal to suddenly be given access to the press led the criminal to believe he or she was in control. Hostages became more valuable to the criminal and could be used to more effect—and "used" frequently meant death. There was also the little known fact that press people had trouble drawing lines, staying objective. Some reporters who covered the police beat for a long time began to think of themselves in police terms and many of them carried weapons. And that, Push thought, watching them, is just what I need—some goddam reporter in back of me with a magnum.

Push knew of a young boy who had taken a .22 revolver and killed his entire family because he wanted to be "on television." Terrorists, Push thought, looking at the reporters, would be nothing without the press.

The TV crew turned their camera lights on and filled the interview corner with glare. Quinsey straightened his tie and moved into the light followed by one of the young on-camera reporters. Push was too far away to hear the questions or answers but knew the classic form Quinsey would follow. No, no need to worry yet . . . one incident . . . several leads being followed . . . arrests imminent. Christ, the reporters knew the answers as well as Quinsey or the rest of them—they could just as well answer their own. And now Quinsey wanted to phony it up by having Push and Dave brief him in front of the cameras— was he insane?

He saw Thorsen sitting with his butt up on the corner of a desk across the squad room from the interview, viewing it with a skeptical eye, and he walked over to him.

"The mighty one speaks," Thorsen said when he got near. "Putting out the word."

"Bullshit."

"That's the word." Thorsen nodded. "Bullshit."

"How's your sex life?"

Thorsen shrugged. "Nothing. Like a wet noodle."

"But with the stewardess . . ."

"I'm like a goat. We screwed all night, raked the sheets, bit the wall. But at home it just hangs there. It's something at home. I can't get it up at home."

Push said nothing. Quinsey was looking at them, the interview was over. For a moment it had seemed that he wanted them to come over, nearly raised his hand to signal them, but good sense took over and he must have then decided against the on-air briefing. Push almost smiled; Quinsey was such a political animal, or thought he was—he'd use his mother to make points. The lights clicked off and Quinsey waited until the reporters had turned away, then beckoned to Push and Dave and pointed to his office. They followed him in.

Lieutenant Quinsey was universally hated by everyone in the department because he was ambitious. He was clean, well-built, had his hair "done," and had a good marriage—he'd been a football star in college and married one of the cheerleaders and they had stayed married and had 2.6 children. He had a nice home out in Aurora, made his car payments, cleaned his nails, didn't swear much, worked as a volunteer in civic groups and had lots of friends on the "outside," civilians who did not work with the police department. He was, in short, the exact opposite of every cop working under him in the detective division and for that reason would probably become a captain and be just as universally hated as he was now except by more influential people.

He pointed to Thorsen to close the door and when it was he smiled—very conscious of the reporters in the other room watching through the glass partitions—and said, "Have you got anything, any single thing to report yet on the cutter case?"

"A good ID on the victim," Thorsen said—he always talked to Quinsey because Push liked to never talk to him. "We're working on it, checking her movements, her friends, co-workers, you know. Like that."

"Nothing."

Thorsen shook his head. "No. Like I said, we've got an ID . . ."

"Nothing," Quinsey repeated. "Like I said. That's why I went up against the press before talking to you. I figured you'd have nothing."

It's been two days, Push thought, and this son of a bitch wants it solved. Push allowed himself to feel angry at his boss, even though he knew that most cases were solved in the first day or two, and frequently if not that soon, then never. Quinsey, he thought, Quinsey just flat pissed him off.

"We're working on it," Thorsen said. "Nuts and bolts."

"I want hourly reports on it, tell me two, three times a day what's happening so I've got something for the press. They're just starting now and they'll get worse as it goes along if we don't solve it."

We, Push thought—if we don't solve it. Hourly reports my ass. Quinsey went back to something on his desk, a signal the interview was over, and the two detectives went back into the squad room.

"He does that because it makes him feel like a supervisor," Push said. "Calls us in while the press are watching. Jesus. We should have pissed on his desk."

Thorsen smiled. "You take it too seriously. Ease with the strain, my boy, ease with the strain."

"Bullshit."

"That's the word." Thorsen nodded. "How do you want to play this?"

Push shook his head and looked away from Thorsen, thought for a moment. "First I'm going to see the department shrink, try to get a profile, then I'll call forensics and see if they got anything off the bags the breasts were in, then go out and start at the airport. Why don't you recheck the ex-husband one time—he could have been lying about the whole thing. Maybe caught her with another guy, went apeshit and dragged her up in the mountains and cut her up . . ."

"That's awfully thin."

"I know it's thin. But it should be checked anyway. If he was bopping with her somebody would know, know if they were still good friends. Give it a check. I think we're going to find it at the airport, but we can't give up on her living area yet. It could be some asshole in the apartment. Check that out, too."

Thorsen nodded, smiled widely, turned to leave and was halfway to the door when Push remembered the stewardess he'd spent the night with. That explained the smile. It didn't matter. Dave had been a long time worrying about his problem and if he could combine work with pleasure . . . well, what the hell.

The reporters were leaving and one of them flipped

the bird to Push and smiled at him. Push nodded. They had long ago given up interviewing Push, knew he would blow the interview, but there was a grudging respect, though they also knew he disliked them. They were aware of his work as a police officer, that he truly worked at it, and some of them even seemed to like him. He waved a finger at them as he left the room.

The nameplate on his desk read Calvin Terrenson but the department psychologist looked to Push almost exactly like a chimpanzee. He had hair but it was cut short and fuzzy, which made his skull look round, domelike, and he had enormous ears that stuck almost straight out to the side.

"How are you," he asked Push, as soon as the door was closed and Push was seated. It was less a question and more a statement. When things had blown up for Push and he had for a time thought of eating his gun he had gone to the shrink. He could not afford a regular doctor so he'd gone to the department psychologist—who was not really a doctor—and without meaning to or knowing it Calvin had furnished some assistance. Push hadn't really thought it would help, but it was a way to get some sick leave and do some serious drinking into numbness while off duty, and that helped more than anything. Or at least he thought it did at the time and everybody had come out on top. The shrink—Push thought of him as the dome-shrink—thought he had helped after six or seven sessions, the booze did help some and Push didn't eat his gun. Now, of course, the psychologist was alluding to Push's difficulties and Push shrugged.

"It's all right."

"So you're not here for yourself . . ."

Push shook his head. He had called and made the appointment without stating the reason. "I'm on a case and need some help—some information."

"What kind of case?"

"We have a cutter."

The psychologist nodded. "I see."

There was a moment of silence.

"I'll need more than that," Calvin said, leaning back in his chair.

"I'm not sure where to start . . ."

"How about sex. Do you know if the cutter is a man or woman?"

"Male. I saw his footprint and he's cutting up women."

"Women," Calvin said quietly, "also cut up women. In fact many mutilators are women . . ."

Push nodded. "I know. But this one is male, I can feel it. Well . . ." he grinned and shrugged, "you know. It just feels that way."

"Tell me everything you have or know about the case."

Push thought for a moment, then started with the beginning, the breast in the airport, the one in Seattle and Betti's body above Idaho Springs. He tried to be as accurate and specific as his memory permitted, including the way the body had been cut up and positioned. It took him a full ten minutes, then he settled back in the wooden chair—he had been disappointed there had never been a couch—and took a breath.

Terrenson had listened intently, not interrupting, until Push was finished. Now he coughed, clearing his throat. "What do you want to know?"

"Everything . . ."

"There are very few places to be specific as yet. You have one body, one method that we don't even know is repeated."

"In general then, give me any information you have that you think even might help."

"A lot of it I'm sure you know . . ."

"Start as if I didn't."

Terrenson sighed. "All right. In general. Mutilators—what you call cutters—are unique in crime and, probably because they usually involve dismemberment in one form or another, seem to hold a particular morbid fascination for people. This interest goes far beyond the seriousness of their crime. The classic example is Jack the Ripper. There are still books and films being done about him though he killed his last victim in, I think, 1888. In all he may have killed five prostitutes in the Whitechapel district of London, probably less. But because he cut them up and mailed parts of them to the police the crime has gained notoriety beyond its impact. As I said, in reality he perhaps killed five women—there are serial killers operating now who have killed over four hundred and they aren't as well known as the story of Jack the Ripper, simply because they don't mutilate."

"I need for you to be more specific than Jack the Ripper," Push said. "I'm not sure that something that old is important."

"But it is. Some cutters kill and mutilate simply for the effect the crimes have on the public. Your cutter, as you term him, might have read a history of Jack the Ripper and wants the same kind of fame. Or notoriety, as it were."

As it were, Push thought. Right. "Do you have a kind of general profile for cut . . . mutilators?"

The psychologist nodded. "There are patterns that seem to hold true. Generally—and this is really wide open—they have had a troubled childhood. Sexual abuse, physical abuse, confinement for long periods of time. These are all things that seem to have contributed to serial killers who mutilate."

Push waited. When nothing further came he prompted. "Is that it?"

Terrenson nodded. "Unless you really want to speculate."

Jesus, Push thought—it's like pulling teeth. "I even want your guesses."

"That's not very professional."

Push wanted to slap him but he forced his voice to be calm. "Look—this son of a bitch is cutting the breasts off live women. Or at least one of them. Give me something. Anything."

"With no recognizable patterns or base to work from, what I say now's all guess work. So let's start with kindergarten stuff. Mutilators tend to be over-achievers, tend to be intelligent—which makes them harder to catch—tend to act very sane, even when they are at their most insane, tend to live oddly settled, proper lives unless they are killing. Many of them travel, either while killing or as part of their work."

Again he stopped, this time frowning in thought.

"What is it?"

"Something about the way you found the body triggered a response in me and I couldn't think of what it was until now."

"So what is it?"

"Ritual . . ." Terrenson mused. He stood suddenly and went to a bookcase on the wall. He scanned it for a moment, then took down a large picture book and opened it. Push rose and went to stand next to him, saw the title at the top of a page.

"Aztecs?"

Terrenson nodded, musing, thumbing through the pages. "Something about the body . . . ahh, here it is."

He pointed to a picture of a stone altar on top of a pyramid. It was a close shot from the top, showing the steps falling away to a dusty square below. On top of the altar—a stone table, really—there was a depression with gutters leading away to the sides and around the edges of the stone altar there were small square niches.

"The Aztecs carried mutilation to probably the most extreme point in history. The Catholic church practiced it some, especially during the Inquisition, but it was more a tool than an aspect of religion. The Aztecs mutilated for the sake of the religion itself."

Push studied the picture. It did not seem familiar to him. The caption said only that it was a sacrificial altar on top of a pyramid, which was named but was not pronounceable.

"Most people know they sacrificed, cut the victims open and took out their hearts. But what isn't common knowledge is that they also cut the victims into pieces, used the blood in further rites, scattered parts of the bodies everywhere." Terrenson looked out the window a moment, thinking. "Bernal Diaz, a soldier with Cortez, wrote in his diary of finding small mountains of just skulls, other heaps of other parts. He numbered the mutilation victims in the tens of thousands and even counting for exaggeration it amounts to a hell of a pile."

"You think this cutter might think he's an Aztec . . ."

Terrenson shook his head. "Not necessarily. We're really reaching here but you said to speculate. When you told me about the way the body of this girl was laid out up at Idaho Springs it struck a chord." He held up the book. "See this altar, the little cubicles around the side? It's thought that they may have put various body parts in the holes after and during the rituals . . ."

"Like he did with the rock pile up at the mine," Push finished, nodding. "I see it now."

"It probably doesn't mean anything, but it's a small connection, at any rate."

"Can I take this book?"

"Of course. Just send it back when you're done."

Push thanked him and left. Like the shrink said, it might not mean anything. But when he'd seen the altar on top of the pyramid, the hair had gone up on the back of his neck. It was as if he'd recognized it, known it from seeing it at Idaho Springs.

He called forensics and got the Melon—a completely bald technician named William Melon whom everybody simply called the Melon for his round head. The Melon was angry, as he always was, and harried, which he always was, and came close to the edge of hanging up on Push.

"Hell no I don't have anything on the bags. Jesus, I've got four techs here and fifty jobs outstanding and you think I'm going to hump it out in two days." He took a breath. "We're scheduled to start on the bags—start on them—in two days. Unless we get more to do. And as you know it will take probably several days to analyze them, go over them, then another day or two to correlate our findings . . ."

He wanted to say more, and more, but Push thanked him and hung up. Melon liked to bitch, but he was damn good at what he did and if he said four or five days he meant four or five days. Push got back into the car and pulled out of the gas station where he'd stopped to call.

Past noon and the heat was again alive. He decided to drive past Scarf's and get a beer and burrito for lunch on his way to the airport. Incredibly the place was empty. Scarf made him a plate of nachos and brought him a dark beer, then leaned on the bar.

"Word is you got a cutter." He wiped at an imaginary damp spot with a rag.

Push nodded. "Looks like it."

"Is it a repeater?"

"No. Not yet. Damn."

"What's the matter?"

"I'm slipping. I forgot to hit the computer and check

on other cities. Christ, that's kid stuff and I forgot it. Just forgot it."

"It happens."

Push left the bar, went to the pay phone and dialed the station, waited and was transferred to the computer. A woman named Helen ran the computer, which was linked by phone lines to a major crime computer network that was in turn linked to the main law enforcement computer, in the F.B.I. headquarters in Washington and Quantico, Virginia. A cop could stop a guy for a ticket and know everything about him before he asked for the driver's license. *If* the system was working. Usually it wasn't. He asked Helen to run a check and see if there were other cutter killings or killings with the same M.O. Then he went back to his burrito.

"You got any leads on it?" Scarf asked. The truth was he missed The Job. Sitting on his ass in back of a bar bored hell out of him and while it helped him avoid the two main retired cop killers—cardiac and suicide—it still bored him.

Push shook his head. He disliked talking about work but recognized Scarf's need. "Nothing really. We're just doing nuts and bolts, turning over rocks and hoping to see something. You know."

"I know." Scarf moved away, satisfied. Push finished his burrito, and went back into the sun, squinting at the light and almost grunting as the heat hit him. The traffic on Colfax was thickening and he made his way slowly towards I-70 and the airport. It was, really, only the second day of the case and already it seemed to be bogging down. Or maybe it was just him. Maybe he was just bogging down.

No, it was Rosa. He'd have to do something about that soon. He wanted to be with her. Live with her. And she wasn't going to go for it and that left him hanging and the truth was he really loved her. Or thought he did. Knew he did. Shit. I love you, he thought.

He drove jaggedly.

How in hell did you investigate an airport?

CHAPTER NINE

Homicides.

There were four others in the Denver area in the two days that Push and Dave had worked on the cutter case.

A drunken father took a swing at his four-year-old son, and the boy's head snapped, cracking his neck so the spinal cord was severed just below the neck trunk. Everything from the waist down stopped, including breathing, and the boy had died in less than two minutes.

A man named Rodriguez found his girl with another man and used a knife to open the man's stomach. The man would live, but in the same motion the knife went into the side of the woman and penetrated her liver, also cutting her lower duodenal tract open. She was in a coma in Denver General and would be dead by morning.

Two bikers had killed a man and a woman on one of the highways out of Denver. A straight rape and murder and a highway patrol officer had come along and caught them. Both so zoned out on crack they didn't know they were arrested until he had them face down on the shoulder.

Four deaths to be investigated. No mysteries, but the law made everything complicated. Four autopsies had to be performed, four sets of forensic packages had to be completed, everything done letter perfect or the perpetrators would get loose on technicalities.

Push drove slowly, remembering something Packard had said. A cop could personally witness a murder, know that it was premeditated, have it on video tape, get a confession from the killer, have twenty other witnesses, carefully read the perpetrator his rights, do all the paperwork perfectly, and the asshole would still skate if he had money, a good lawyer and time.

Push parked at the airport and walked through the afternoon heat to the administration building. He had decided to start with administration out of courtesy, then go to security, then back to the airline that had employed Betti Fencer, which is where he thought he'd get the most help. Administration knew nothing about the small people, the working people, and security was all rent-a-cops who did nothing more than look for suspicious luggage.

He found the administration offices upstairs and was kept waiting for seven minutes—he counted—until he was finally shown in to Mr. McGanser, a thin man in a gray suit and gray designer glasses who sat at a large desk.

"I need to know more about the airport," Push told him after settling into a chair. "The mechanics of it."

"You mean the planes, all of it?"

"No. I guess what I need to know is about all the people—the employees. Are they all screened, and if so where can I get into the records?"

McGanser hesitated. "We . . . have some difficulty here. I mean we can't just let you have access to all the records on all the employees. Not without some . . . authorization of some kind."

"I can get a court order," Push said.

"Actually, I don't think you can," McGanser said, his voice slightly smug, "for something this vague."

Push studied him, anger rising. "The way I see it, you can cooperate openly and we'd be grateful or I can ask a friend of mine in immigration and records to start running our own screening process on your whole system—which would tie things up for weeks, worse if you got any illegals working here."

McGanser blanched, swallowed.

Push eased his voice. "Listen, we have good reason to believe that what happened to Betti Fencer had something to do with the airport. She worked through here, spent a lot of time here, and it's possible that some other employee at the airport knows something about her murder. You wouldn't want to impede any investigation of that, would you?"

"No, no." McGanser smiled, eager to help. "Not at all. But I'll have to clear it through Mr. Stanton. There is another problem, however."

"What's that?"

"Well, airport services are provided by independent subcontractors. There's security, maintenance, custodial—all furnished by different companies who keep all their own employee records. We simply don't have a large, central office with all the records. And then there are the airlines—each of them has its own administration and each category of employee has its own union. I'm afraid it's all a lot more complicated than you seem to think."

"Probably. But if I have your cooperation and maybe a letter asking for others to help me it should go a lot easier."

McGanser considered it, then called Stanton, told him what Push wanted, hung up and nodded. "Mr. Stanton said we could give you a memo of cooperation but he asks that you keep the matter as quiet as possible. What with hijackings and terrorism, airports have enough problems. Are you sure it's not terrorist activity?"

"I'm not sure of anything. But terrorism is unlikely. Usually there are demands, or at least admissions—this is all too secret." Except, he thought, that bit about sending the breasts off in bags. Could that be some warped terrorist?

"Because if it's terrorism or you even think it is we could call in the F.B.I. . . ."

Push shook his head. "Not yet. Let's see where it goes first." No F.B.I. he thought. He hated to work with them. They were so . . . so neat. Everything in small packages, catalogued, clean and neat. They didn't know the street and usually didn't get publicly involved in a case until they were pretty sure it was going to be solved, then took full credit for it. If they jumped into the middle of a case they almost invariably messed it up.

Push stood. "If you'll give me that memo I'll start with maintenance and custodial services."

"All together you're dealing with several hundred— no, over a thousand employees." McGanser called his secretary in and ordered the memo. "You have your work cut out for you."

"It's a start . . ."

He went to maintenance, showed them the memo, and was immediately given a master list of all their employees. They had all been cleared through national security computers but he took the names to give to Helen at the police computer center. Sometimes national security didn't cover smaller things—like sex hangups or links with religious cults or cross-references to abuse situations.

Next he hit the main custodial office for the airport and found another list for the computer, which they released easily—afraid to anger administration. Riding down an escalator with the two lists he smiled and thought, hell, this is easy. Just keep getting master lists and feeding them into computers. Something should pop. The marvels of high-tech.

He should have known better.

When he started on the airlines he ran into a brick wall.

He went first to Transair—Betti Fencer's employer—explained that they had positive identification on the body and asked for a list of employees.

"I'm afraid not." The flight attendant supervisor— the same one he'd spoken to before—stopped him cold.

"I need it to cross-reference information," he said.

"If need be I can get a court order but I thought it would be simpler if we all cooperated . . ."

"Then you'll have to get a court order. The flight attendants' names and addresses are confidential and if I let them out their union would tear us apart." She shook her head. "You have no idea what you're asking. If we released that list to you they could strike the airline. We could be closed down in an hour."

"How about the pilots?"

"Worse. Even more difficult. Not only will you have to get a court order but they'll fight the order. The pilots' union is very strong and they could fight it for years."

"Look, all I'm trying to do is find out who killed Betti Fencer. I won't use the list for anything else . . ."

"That doesn't matter. I'm not allowed. Period. I'm sorry, really I am. I—we want to catch whoever did this to Betti at least as much as you do. But there are very rigid controls."

He tried to find the second door. Old Packard used to say—usually after raising up on one cheek and farting—that when they slammed one door it almost always blew another one open. Where was the second door here? Records. Yes. Other records. Money. No, health. Health records. That would be a list of names. Insurance. Company insurance. "Could you tell me the name of the company that provides health insurance for the employees?"

She smiled, suddenly, and nodded. "I see what you're doing. It's Grafton Mutual Assurance—and I'll write the address and phone number of the Denver office for you. I doubt they'll help, but good luck. Like I said, we all want to catch whoever did this . . ."

He left, going to the other airlines, spending the rest of the afternoon running into a series of brick walls—the unions dominated the employees. But he did find out that Grafton furnished the health insurance for most of the airlines and he got the names of the insurance companies for those that Grafton didn't. By the time he finished with the airlines it was four o'clock and he had wanted to be at Harry's junkyard at four when the employees left.

Back at the station he'd looked at the file on the man Cartier wanted taken down—a guy named Strunk, street name of Juniper—and Cartier had been right. The son of a bitch would hurt somebody soon and the law had gotten in the way as Cartier had said. He was guilty as hell but Mattson kept him loose, found technical holes, kept him on the street to steal and pay Mattson his enormous fees. Having an expensive lawyer was like being a drug addict. Juniper had to steal to pay Mattson and Mattson would get him off so he could steal to pay Mattson again. There was no end to it.

The problem, he thought, walking through the parking lot at the airport to get to his car, was that Juniper was like other thieves. The more he stole, the more he got away with it, the cockier and meaner he became. On some of Juniper's last jobs he'd threatened the victims with a knife. The classic case, Push thought—the son of a bitch was wired to kill somebody. First assault, then harder assault, probably two or three rapes—or more if the women didn't go through the endless misery of convicting the bastard—and finally he'd kill somebody. Then, if everything worked right, he'd catch a little time but then he'd be back on the street and do it again. A classic case. Many priors, tons of arrests, and he hadn't been convicted for years. But there were enough early convictions so that if Push set up a solid case Juniper would do hard time.

And that was where Harry came in.

Harry would provide the solid case

Interiors
Two

Choices.

It was time again. They were calling him again, soon after the last one.

There were two of them this time. Two different women had been covered by the light and he had to make a choice and that had happened only once before, in Rome, and he hated making the choice.

One was a stewardess, like the last one, but she was close. So close to him, closer than the last time, and it would be wrong to draw attention to himself so soon. If they took him now, took him too soon, he would never finish his mission and so he decided not to take the stewardess with the light over her head.

The other one was the car rental girl. His wife had kept the car and didn't answer the phone, and he had gone to rent a car, still thinking about the stewardess with the light over her head. He had looked up and there it was, glowing over the rental girl as she smiled at him and made out the form.

Perfect.

It was amazingly easy. But then it always was. He had been given tall, good looks, he knew that, and then there was the uniform. He looked good in the uniform but it was more what the uniform meant than how he looked; it meant money, prestige, position and security. Often women came up to him and pressed pieces of paper with their phone numbers and addresses into his hand and one of those women, back in Pennsylvania, one of those had had the light on her and had practically offered herself for the ritual.

It was the same with the rental girl. She had given him the smile and the movement of the hips that meant so little but seemed to mean so much and he answered her smile because she had the glow and he felt the genuine affection, almost love, he felt for them when they had the glow.

What time do you get off, he asked, and she had answered two o'clock.

And that had been that. He had the needle and Valium and knife with him because he always took it on trips and he picked her up at two in the rental car, picked her up out of the crowd around the baggage area exit and she slid into the seat and he pushed the needle into her arm as they left the booth of the rental parking lot.

She had of course jumped and started to say something but he grabbed her with his free arm and held her for a moment and the drug hit fast—he was amazed at how fast the drug worked—and her head slumped over on the last word, slumped before he finished and removed the needle, and she was unconscious, her breathing short and ragged.

It was better this way. Sometimes he had let them talk before injecting them, to relax them. Twice he had gone to bed with them and given them that small thing before the injection but he had stopped that because it had been harder to do the second part after being in bed with them, made them less pure for the ritual.

He braked suddenly when he turned onto Airport Road, to avoid a scuffed-up tan car that got the last of the light, and the car rental girl slammed forward loosely into the dashboard. She had not fastened her belt when she got in and he reached across now and buckled her. They must not be damaged. It was a critical part, a rule—they must not be damaged before he removed their clothes and prepared them. He had read that in the ancient times the priests took only the most beautiful, the bravest and the best. If they were flawed, if the ceremony was flawed, it diminished him and he would not be diminished.

He drove slowly, carefully, heading onto I-70 west up into the mountains. There was a small road back into the pines not too far from Evergreen, above the Brook Forest Inn. The road was drivable without a four-wheel drive—much better than last time when he had to use the Jeep wagon. It was better at night but he had done some of them in the light of day and it was still acceptable. Not as good, but still acceptable.

Next to him the girl took a long, deep breath, shuddered slightly, and then her breathing seemed to stop. He did not know the right dosages for the different weights and he was distressed for a moment thinking she was gone but in a few seconds she seemed to jerk and her breathing resumed, although jagged and patchy.

It was a sign, he thought. A good sign that she started breathing again. They had sent her back from the edge. A good sign. Things would go well.

He drove evenly, letting his professional reflexes handle the car.

It would go well.

CHAPTER
TEN

Harry Swenson was a short, tightly-muscled balding man of forty who owned a junkyard along the railroad tracks in the southwest end of Denver. Or at least from the outside it looked like any other junkyard. And Harry did a hell of a business buying and selling steel, copper and junked cars that he crushed and cubed up in a machine, most of the money tax-free because junk is so hard to keep track of; in fact Harry could have lived really well just off the junk business, really well on just what he managed to hide from the IRS. He had put a son and daughter through Harvard on the money from junk. He owned a huge house in Lakewood, full of expensive chrome and plastic furniture and white carpets, complete with an enormous pool, and he had a wife who was forty but looked twenty-seven through the miracles of modern surgery—all paid for with the money from junk.

But the junkyard was just a front. Outside it looked like a standard junkyard, an old concrete-block building surrounded by hunks of rusting metal and pipe, with two greasy, unbelievably dirty men burning the guts out of starter motors to get at the copper or using a weigh scale that was probably fixed, everything a grubby gray covered with smokey dirt and dust.

Out back, in an enclosed cage, were two Dobermans that—as Harry put it—could ". . . eat a goddam Buick and shit Volkswagens." They growled and barked as Push got out of the car. Every night when the junkyard was locked up and the chain link fence sealed the Dobermans were let out to patrol until daylight. Only one time had anybody climbed the fence and gotten into the compound—an old wino looking for metal to swap for sneaky pete—and as Harry put it, smiling, "They could have buried the son of a bitch in four places when the dobies got done with him."

In front of the building, next to where Push parked the unmarked police car that everybody in this neighborhood knew was a police car, was parked a spotless white Cadillac.

And inside the building, Push knew, was a suite of offices filled with plush furniture, fifteen or twenty employees all busy at computer terminals and desks, all running a financial empire that only Harry really understood. He did import, export, stocks and bonds, money market work, some things that Push did not want to think about too closely—everything and anything to make money and he made a lot of money. Push figured millions.

Harry was not the sort of person Push would normally know. He would normally know people who frequented Scarf's place, or hookers and pimps and drug addicts and killers or Dave Thorsen. Not people with seven figure incomes.

But at one time Harry's son had gotten sideways in his life. Push remembered him as a tall, skinny kid with pimples and a perpetually worried look, but that might have been because Push found him in the tank at the jail with winos, street grunge and a dirty neck biker who wouldn't quit looking at the kid's skinny little ass. The kid was terrified. He had been clipped with a plastic bag full of pot, which wouldn't have done much to hurt him—it was a smokable amount only. A misdemeanor. But the kid had been with somebody in the car who was carrying a heavy bag of coke—a seller—and that made the kid an accessory to a felony. Push was working vice then and made the bust on a target of opportunity hit. He'd been staking out a larger seller and happened on the deal and made the arrest.

It was not that the kid would have done hard time. Clearly he was small stuff and would have gotten at most some county time or walked with a fine and probation. But Push had taken pity on him. He was just so damn scared—too scared even to call his father or a lawyer—and after four hours in the tank Push had used arresting officer's discretion to let the kid go. And that had been the end of it.

Or so he thought at the time. Two weeks later he received an envelope containing ten crisp one-hundred-dollar bills and a note on a letterhead saying the kid would never fuck up again and thanking him for his discretion, signed by Harry.

It hadn't been a bribe. The action was already done. And Push knew at least fifty cops who would have taken the money. His partner at the time, a wizened cop named Clairborn, told him to keep it. But he was uncomfortable with it and drove to the address on the letterhead, the junkyard, and returned the money to Harry, which surprised the hell out of both of them.

They had, in the strange way that life moves, become good friends. Perhaps because they had absolutely nothing in common. Harry was rich, Push was lucky to make the light bill; Harry was intense, driven, Push floated and rolled with it; Harry had a family, a life, Push had motel rooms and Rosa. Sometimes.

Push opened the door and went into the outer office. It was clean, but still looked primarily like a junkyard office. Grimy windows and an old hardwood desk with a distributor cap on it holding pencils. At the desk sat a gray-haired lady—Push knew she was Harry's sister, a widow who ran the junkyard portion of the business—who seemed to be someone's older aunt.

"Hello Gladys," Push said, smiling. "He in?"

Gladys nodded without looking up. She had a pencil in her hair and another one in her hand and was studying some kind of manifest or invoice. Her voice was hard. She was all business and people who thought in stereotypes of little old ladies should have met her, Push thought; when it came to business she was a barracuda. He'd once seen her nearly tear the heart out of a trucker who tried to short her on a load of iron he was delivering. "Back in the offices. Go on in."

Push went through a nondescript door to the left of Gladys' desk and stopped inside. It always surprised him, coming through the door. He'd been here ten or twelve times and it always surprised him. It was like going to a different world. He entered a large bay with ten desks, at each of which sat a keyboard operator punching away at a computer terminal.

At the other end of the bay was another door—the door to Harry's office—and it opened as he looked at it. Gladys, of course, would have called Harry and told him Push was here.

"Goddam," Harry said, bursting from the office. "What the hell do you need now?"

He was wearing a gray suit with a vest, which matched the gray in his hair at the temples—he was bald on top—and on his fingers were several gold rings. A gold watch glittered at his wrist. He was smiling, with even white teeth. Push looked down at his own clothes—a sport coat that looked as if he'd driven over it, scuffed shoes, mustard-stained pants, or at least the stain was from something that had been yellow, he couldn't remember eating mustard, worn for two days, tie worn for two weeks—and felt like a slob.

"What do you mean, need?" Push asked, holding out his hand. "Can't I just come to pass the time of day?"

Harry shook his hand, then hugged him. "You're such a lying bastard . . . come on in the office and have a drink."

He dragged Push into the office and closed the door. Harry's wife had decorated the room with white carpet deep enough to hunt rhinos in, a walnut desk that cost more than the budget of some small countries, modern paintings that looked spit on, and a sculpture made of chromed pipe and plastic. Everything dripped of money.

Push slid into a chair that seemed to be made of air and plastic. "I can't get over how nice your office is."

Harry filled two glasses with some amber liquid from a side bar and handed one to Push. He tasted it and found bourbon with some ice.

"My office looks like a whorehouse from 2001 and you know it," Harry said, amiably. "My wife's taste is far out. Jesus, you should see what she's done to the pool. Some kind of goddam sculpture that looks like it eats meat. I think she's screwing the artist and he talked her into it. Three grand. Goddam piece of shit . . ."

Push laughed. Harry's wife loved him. Completely. They had paid some dues in their lives but were very happy now. Still, his office did look like a futuristic whorehouse.

"My kid," Harry said suddenly. "Patrick. The little shit just passed the bar. How about that?"

"Give him my congratulations . . ."

Harry was suddenly serious. "It never would have happened except for you. You know that."

"That's old stuff. Let's drop it."

"Just so you know."

"It's all right . . ."

"So." Harry took a drink. "What do you need? Money?"

It was a joke between them since Push had turned

down the hundred dollar bills and Push smiled. "No. I need a little help with an asshole."

He quickly told Harry the story of Juniper, how he wanted him off the street, how he would soon be doing heavier things. "It's simple, really," he finished. "I want you to swear out a complaint saying he busted into your place and took some money. A burglary cop will process the complaint and Juniper will do time."

Harry looked at him, studied him for a half a minute. "This guy must be bad."

Push shrugged. "I know worse. But we can stop him before he rapes, or kills."

"Will it go to court?"

"Absolutely not. Mattson is his lawyer. They'll bargain it down and he'll go to the slammer for a while. He's had enough priors that we can take him out for eight or nine years . . ."

"Why do you do this?"

"What do you mean? It's my job."

"Shit."

Push sat quietly. There was not a way to tell him. Years of watching assholes skate, years of watching the lowest form of life on the planet, years of watching rapers and killers and cutters and slashers and abusers, years of watching takers and never givers, rapers of more than bodies, rapers of life, killers of souls, enders of civilization . . . how to tell Harry? How to tell anybody? He did it now the way a slug moved, did it because he had to, did it because it was, in the end, his job. The Job.

"You put your ass on the line," Harry said gently,

"right on the line to take some guy off the street for eight years. Quit it. Quit it now and come to work for me. I'll pay you twice what you're getting and give you a rocker on a porch when you're done."

Push said nothing. Waited.

"You're fucking nuts, you know that?" Harry shook his head. "Right out of the tree fucking nuts."

"Will you do the complaint?"

"Of course. You knew I would."

"I owe you one."

"No. You don't. I think I owe you. I think maybe we all owe you. I mean you really care . . . ahh, shit. Never mind. Let's go get piss drunk and look at barmaids for a while."

They jumped in the white Caddy and went to a place called, simply, The Pit. It was all wood and leather and coarse flooring. Sometimes some of the Denver Broncos came there to drink and there were scars on the walls and bent barstools from the last time they'd broken loose. Push started with beer but soon went back to bourbon and Harry stayed with bourbon and in two hours they had achieved Harry's purpose—they were both piss drunk, maudlin, ready to solve the world's problems and incapable of reasonable thought.

They went out of the bar barely walking—both squinting and weaving in the sudden daylight. Harry drove back to the junkyard, escorted Push to his car, and then returned to his office to let Gladys run the rest of the day while he tried to drink ". . . enough black coffee so I can find my ass with both hands." Push sat in the police car for at least three minutes trying to get the key in the slot. At last he made it, started the car and peered out the windshield into the afternoon brightness.

He had to call Rosa. He knew that. He and Harry had decided he should call Rosa and tell her he wanted to marry her and to hell with her husband and the hundred thou a year. He had to call her. But first, he thought, backing out of the parking area by the junkyard and completely across the street and into some garbage cans against a wall—first he had to drive by his ex-wife's place.

Get that out of the way.

Then call Rosa.

Interiors
Three

Some part of it was wrong.

Some part of his thinking was incorrect or she was not pure, not acceptable by them. Whatever the reason it all fell apart on him.

He found the place back in the trees above Evergreen well enough, following the curving road until it became two ruts. He'd been there on a hike once, knew it led to an old mine, and was certain no people would be there to bother him while he performed the ritual. It was important that he be undisturbed for the ritual. Everything had to run smoothly for the special one to be received.

But no sooner had he placed her reverently on the deep grass at the edge of the road in a clearing—no sooner had he taken her clothes off to make her pure and made the first removing cut, then her eyes snapped open and she screamed and started to thrash around on the ground. Somehow the drug had partially worn off.

It was a high-pitched scream, a keening scream

mixed with spit and horror and it absolutely terrified him.

He poked with the knife, poked and poked all up and down her body to end the screaming, and finally when the knife went through her neck it stopped, wavered off in gurgles as the blood filled her throat and she died. But of course it was all ruined.

All ruined.

The body was all a shambles, holes all over it, and he was covered with blood from the splashing and squirting. He jumped in the car and drove away, leaving the body and thinking of nothing except getting away. Getting away.

He stopped near a stream before entering the highway and washed as best he could—washed the knife and threw away his rubber gloves and tried to clean his clothing. But there was blood on his uniform coat and it wouldn't come out, which meant he would have to burn it and get a new one. It couldn't be left around to be seen or found by those who would not understand the importance of his work.

And on top of all of it his wife had something scheduled for late afternoon, some dinner party or other. She was always doing that to him. Scheduling things he hadn't planned on—he'd have to sneak in and change and get ready for the party. No, first he'd have to change, then take the rental car back and have his wife take him home, and then get ready for the party or whatever the hell it was she was doing to him. Everything was getting so complicated.

Shit.

It was all going bad.

CHAPTER ELEVEN

They had to hurry.

Bill Clearven worked at the Dew Drop Inn in Evergreen as a cook on the evening shift and only had one hour for lunch. Sandy Faren was a waitress at the same place and sparks had turned to flame between them once when she put an order in for tacos and their eyes had met. Bill was, unfortunately, married to a woman named Wendy and Sandy was married to a man named Carl but true workplace love will out and they had found that if they took their lunch at the same time and drove Bill's Ford Escort like hell out into the woods around Evergreen and she threw a leg over him in the front seat he would get one and she would get multiple orgasms during their lunch hour. They would then go back to work the rest of the night on rubber legs, Bill nearly face down on the grill and Sandy smiling even at the assholes who didn't tip.

But they had to hurry.

This evening they got in trouble because the place they normally stopped—a cut-off on the creek—was being repaired by a road crew putting in a new culvert. Bill tried two more spots that proved to be driveways.

"Maybe we'd better pass today," Sandy said, continuing to rub her hand between his legs. He felt his temples about to explode and it was all he could do to keep the car on the road. "Maybe we should wait . . ."

"Today is Friday," he said, gritting his teeth. "If we wait we'd have to wait until Monday. I don't know if I can stand to wait that long."

Just then they came on a twin rut road that turned to the left and Bill whipped the little Escort off the highway, across a small stream and back into the trees where there was a clearing.

"Perfect!" he said, grabbing for his fly and moving his seat back. Sandy dropped her bikini panties in a single, practiced motion and their faces glued together as she climbed over the partition between the seats and straddled him. It was awkward but they had done it before and knew just where to place each limb to get the job done and in seconds she was moaning, with her mouth against Bill's ear, while he closed his eyes and ground his teeth together trying to hold back.

It was possible that Sandy's scream caused permanent damage to Bill's ear. It was a primal scream, not just loud enough to deafen, but filled with some ancient terror, some genetic terror that cut through more than Bill's ear, seared through his brain and into his heart.

"Eeeeeeeeeeeaaaaaaarrrrgggg!"

Bill slammed his head away, tried to get a hand to his ear, and when his eyes opened he saw what Sandy had seen and started a matching scream.

At the passenger side window, pressed against the glass, was a woman's face. Or what had once been a woman's face. Now it was a mask, a chopped and bloody mask of horror smearing bloodily across the glass. The mouth was open in an attempt to speak, to scream, to beg, to cry, but only silence came out. Beneath the mouth where the throat should have been was a bubbling open wound, spewing a froth of air and blood like an obscene second mouth, and as Sandy and Bill watched, frozen, the face slid down the window and dropped out of sight— ending two marriages and any hope of future erections for Bill until he had spent several thousand dollars on therapy.

Dave found Push at Push's apartment building, sitting in the parking area in the lot assigned to the manager. Push had been thinking of going in, but he was too drunk to open either the car door or the apartment door, keys and holes being what they were, so he'd just passed out in the car.

Dave had gone to Harry's, found there that Push and Harry had gotten drunk together—Gladys told him because Harry was sleeping it off in his office. Dave had then driven by Push's ex-wife's place, and finally gone back to Push's apartment.

"Jesus," he said, opening the car door. "You smell like a dump."

Push opened one eye, identified Dave, closed the eye. "I smell correct, correct, correct . . ."

"Correct for somebody who shit his pants."

"That may have happened. I am drunk. I used to know a wino who shit his pants all the time. We made rookies take him in. Can't remember his name now, what was his name? Oh, yeah, Richard. We always made the rookies take Richard in 'cause he always shit his pants. So maybe I'm becoming a wino and I have shit my pants . . ."

Dave ignored the words running one on each other out of Push's mouth and took his arm, pulled him from the car. A couple got out of a car in the next stall and stared at them and Dave gave them the cop look—the look that made people turn away instantly and not meddle. All cops have it. It's a look of complete power, a look that means if you mess with the bull you get the horn. The couple turned away instantly and Dave pulled Push out into the hot sunshine. Push staggered, and leaned against the car. The heat smashed him and he started to throw up, his forehead against his arm, the vomit running down the side of the car.

Dave waited patiently for him to finish, then took his arm again.

"Come on. I've got six cups of coffee and a burrito in my car."

"I need a beer more."

"The hell you do. You've got to get straight. And damn soon."

Even through the fog Push sensed the urgency in

Dave's voice. "What's happening? Old Quince pissed off?"

"No. The son of a bitch missed one. The cutter left one alive and she's at Denver General. They don't think she's going to make it but say she might regain consciousness before she dies. We want to be there if she does."

"Oh yes, oh Jesus yes we do." Push lurched out of Dave's hands and made for the car. "You bet your ass we do . . ." He stopped suddenly and threw up again, standing with his hands on his knees.

"If something round and furry comes up . . ." Dave didn't finish the joke.

"Yeah. I know. It's my asshole." Push stood and wiped his mouth with the back of his hand. "Don't ever drink with Harry. The son of a bitch is hollow."

"He's passed out in his office," Dave said. "In worse shape than you are." He got in the car and started the engine. Push slid in the passenger side. Between them on the seat were two carry-out cartons with burritos and coffee and Push took a burrito and a cup of coffee at once. Food and coffee had stopped many a drunk. He drank a cup, still hot, as fast as possible, then took a large bite of burrito and was feeling better before they left the parking area of his apartment.

"Roll your window down," Dave said, turning onto the street. "I mean Jesus, you smell awful."

She lay in intensive care hooked to tubes and wires and respirators. Some technician or nurse had thoughtfully spread part of a gown over her pubic area, but from the waist up and thigh down she was nude. Her eyes were wide open and her body was a mass of wounds. Cuts and punctures and abrasions. They had bandaged the wound at her throat and some of the worst body wounds, but the rest of her was bare and looked—to Push—absolutely ravaged. It was the first word that came to mind.

A young doctor came in. "You're the police? Here on the murder?"

Push shook his head. "Not yet. Not if she's still alive. It's not murder until she dies."

"Then it's murder. She's dead, clinically, we're just keeping the respirator going until some relative gets here to tell us to unplug her or to authorize us to use some of her organs. She's gone, been gone for over half an hour." The doctor shook his head. He had curly hair, tight around his temples, and a boyish look that must make him the target for every young woman who came to the hospital. "Amazingly strong, for such a small woman. To pull herself up on the car that way and look in the window. She must have been running on pure adrenalin by that time."

Push looked down at her. He had an almost irresistible impulse to hold her hand, pat her and tell her it would be all right. Of course it wouldn't be all right. Not ever. Not for her. Her arms and hands were a mass of wounds—defense cuts. She had been conscious when he did this. Fighting the son of a bitch. The other woman had been drugged. There had been no defense cuts on her arms. This one was cut all to hell.

"We . . . uhh . . . need her name," the doctor said, cutting into his thinking. "For our records."

Push looked at Dave who shook his head. "Nothing. She was nude so we didn't get any ID and we haven't got any prints yet. Been too busy. If prints would help. They might not if she isn't on record somewhere."

"Did she say anything?" Push asked the doctor. "Any sounds at all?"

The doctor shook his head. "Just some hissing through the throat wound. Not sound, just exhalation. There were no words, nothing you could use. Well, if you'll excuse me, I've got to go call the television station . . ."

He started to walk away and had taken three steps before Dave stopped him. "What do you mean, call the television station?"

The doctor turned. "When she first came in that television reporter was here—the one with the thick glasses?—on another story. He had a cameraman with him and they got pictures of her when she came in. But they took off with the story while she was still alive and there was some hope. After that we found massive internal bleeding and also found that the shock was terminal, if not the loss of blood. She had been stabbed at least twenty and perhaps as many as fifty times with a long-bladed knife of some kind." This last he said in a technical voice, as if testifying in court. "Anyway, I'd better call the station and correct the story, tell them she's dead."

Dave looked at Push, raised his eyebrows. Push nodded.

"But she isn't dead," Push said. "Not really. Not as long as the respirator is keeping her system going."

The doctor shook his head. "No. She's gone, really."

"No." Push insisted. "She's still alive. Don't tell them she's dead."

The doctor studied him.

Push said nothing. Most of it, he thought—most of it is knowing when to keep your goddam mouth shut.

"You're going to use her for bait." It was less a question than a statement of fact.

"You know the person who did this is a maniac, don't you? I mean he stabbed her over and over after trying to cut off one of her breasts. You know what you're asking me—to put the whole hospital at risk . . ."

"This is the second woman," Push said. "It's almost certainly the same killer and he's done one other woman that we know about. Maybe more. We're not asking you to lie, or do anything wrong. Just don't call them. As long as the respirator is going she could be called alive. Just don't change the story. Yet."

The doctor hesitated, clearly troubled by Push's request.

"And there's almost no risk," Dave said, lying. He had such a sincere face his lies were almost always believed. Push couldn't lie half as well as Dave and always let his partner do the serious lying. Like now. There was definite risk. "We'll have undercover operators all through the hospital. Down on the main floor, in the halls, out in the parking lot. We'll have this place covered so thick you couldn't get a flea in here without being seen."

All lies. All professionally told lies. The truth was they couldn't tell the department because it was against policy to use live people as lures—even dead live people. It was also against policy to set up such a definitely risky operation in a place like a hospital where there was a chance of danger to so many innocent people. Even if they could have told the department Quinsey wouldn't authorize the operation because he would be afraid of the outcome and having it come down on his head. So they had to lie to make it work. And because they couldn't tell the department they wouldn't have help.

It would be just the two of them covering the whole hospital.

Which was nothing new to either of them.

The young doctor bought it. He held back for another ten seconds, thinking, then he shrugged. "If you're sure you'll have it covered from every angle . . ."

"No sweat," Dave said, his eyes sincere and forthright. "We'll call the station right now and have the undercover team get ready. They'll have to start trickling in—if they all come at once it might arouse suspicion."

Almost too much, Push thought, wincing inwardly. Dave was carrying it too far. Trickle in. Shit. But the doctor nodded and went back to his rounds.

"Think it will work?" Push asked. His hangover was starting to assume gigantic proportions as the booze wore completely off and the taste in his mouth from the coffee, burritos and vomit took over. He felt like puking again. And the hospital smell didn't help.

"Not a chance. But we had to try it, right?"

"Right."

"If the son of a bitch comes he's an idiot."

"Or crazy."

"Or both."

Dave took a notebook out of his pocket. "There's some more nuts and bolts shit to do. The couple who found her—or I guess the couple she found—are down at headquarters waiting to be questioned. They called an ambulance and the ambulance brought her straight here so the Jefferson County Sheriff's department hasn't been notified yet unless the ambulance crew or the hospital did so. I don't think that happened so we've got to call them, then go up there and do a crime scene with them. We've also got to question the couple—how do you want to break it down?"

Push looked at his watch. There was some kind of stain blocking out the digital numbers. Jesus, had he puked on his watch? "It's five-thirty. I'll go question the couple and then boogie back here in case they put it on the six o'clock news and he makes a move. I know it probably won't happen, but we should be here just in case. And I wouldn't be worth a shit on the crime scene. My brain isn't working right yet."

Dave nodded. "I'll be back here as soon as I finish up the crime scene with the Jeff county people. Catch you later."

He left and Push realized suddenly that they had been standing over the girl's body, which was hissing and whooshing with the respirator, the chest rising and falling artificially as the machine pumped air into the dead cavity of her lungs. It seemed like his whole life was standing over bodies and talking.

He didn't even know her name.

He was halfway to the door when he remembered that Dave had brought him in Dave's car and so he didn't have a vehicle. He'd have to get a cab back to his apartment and then drive to the station to talk to the couple.

So, he thought, why should things go smoothly?

Interiors
Four

It was not possible she was still alive.

Everything had gone so smoothly after the initial debacle of the ritual. He had gotten home and changed without being seen—he lived only half an hour from where he had left the body, or what he thought was the body. His wife had been at the beauty parlor. When she came back they had taken the rental car to the airport and then returned home to get ready for the party.

So smoothly until the evening party. They were at a friend's house. He'd just been promoted from flight engineer to second officer and they were celebrating his status change, joking about his having been a "plumber," the nickname for flight engineers.

He had walked through a bedroom to use a bathroom and they had the television going on a stand and just as he passed, just then he looked up and there was the picture of the woman in the hospital.

He stopped, stopped everything. His movement,

his breath, his thinking, his brain, his life—everything stopped and he stared at the screen.

It was not possible.

But there it was. She was in a hospital, in intensive care, the woman he'd left in the clearing not three, no, four hours ago. Left absolutely dead. There she was with tubes and doctors and nurses working on her, hooked to support systems.

Alive.

"She is not conscious and her condition is very critical," the doctor was saying, "but we seem to have stabilized it and there is some hope. We have a good intensive care staff here at Denver General. Now please, move the camera away and let us get to work."

And it was gone. The news moved on to a story about Cherry Creek Reservoir being too dry and he wanted to shake the set, shake the world and get the story back, see it again. He looked to the left and right, wanted to ask somebody if they'd seen it, but he was alone in the room with the set. He couldn't believe it.

She was alive. She was alive and knew him and she might regain consciousness and be able to talk and talk and talk . . .

He had to be cautious about this. Very careful. Very cool. There could be no connection between him and the woman on the screen. None. He had always been so careful to not have a connection. Not one. And not once in all the times he'd let the red out—he did not count but there were many, back in Cleveland, then Toronto and Chicago and Seattle and now here, many times—and not once had he left one alive.

But she had been there. He had seen it. It was the same girl he left in the clearing.

And she was alive.

Where was it? Oh yes, alive at Denver General Hospital.

Oh god, he thought, panic taking him. He could see it all leaving him, all that he was—see it all being blown apart by this one mistake. Huge home, investments, family, his career; all of it destroyed by this one small error in judgment, one incorrect ritual.

Then his wife had found him standing in the bedroom, shaking, holding his drink and shaking. She had put her arm around his waist and called him back to the party and he'd had to go, had to go, had to go.

He looked once more at the screen as he left the room. They were showing the weather. He knew the weather. An occluded front was coming but it wouldn't matter because they could fly over it. The 727 could fly over any weather problems they had. There might be shear but he would know that as well. He had a sixth sense about shear as some of his friends had. He could not explain it. But if certain weather patterns developed he could almost sense if there would be shear. He knew weather.

Denver General, the man had said.

Oh god, he thought. Oh-god-oh-god-oh-god . . .

CHAPTER
TWELVE

Push drove slowly back to the hospital, chewing on a Wendy's with everything, trying to drink a malt and eat while he drove because he still needed food to fight the hangover and he wouldn't be able to eat in the hospital.

Questioning the couple had proved fruitless. For one thing they were so absolutely terrified they could barely speak without stuttering and Push thought it had to do with the body but found there was more. The whole thing had been done wrong. They were brought to the police station by—of all people—the ambulance driver, and let off out front, had to walk in and report what had happened and who they were. Heads would roll for that, for not following proper interview procedures, for not getting a car out to the crime scene before principal witnesses were taken away, for not establishing any questioning base. Almost nothing had been done right and it left major holes concerning the couple.

What really had the couple frightened was that they

were on the road getting a quicky and they were afraid their spouses would find out. Which of course they would. Though Push lied and told them everything would be in the "... strictest confidence." When and if things went to court later they would have to testify. Both of them. And explain in great detail just why they were on the road, what they were doing, in exactly what position they were when the woman's face appeared at the car window.

But Push let them live in peace for the moment. The press had descended on the station and there were several messages on his desk to contact Quinsey, but he ignored both Quinsey and the press. Quinsey could handle the reporters for now, put them off with vague comments—he was good at that. Being vague. Son of a bitch had a vague brain, Push thought, smiling. He'd have to tell that to Dave. Quinsey had vague-brain.

He had let the couple out the back entrance, through the holding cells, to give them a head start on the press. They'd undoubtedly get nailed by the bastards anyway—at their homes if no other place, which would blow their identity. But they were grateful for small favors and had no idea of the carnage that was about to enter their lives. In a very real measure Push had great pity on them. He was doing the same thing with Rosa and although he didn't give a good goddam if they were caught or not, Rosa sure as hell did. She would be horrified to be in such a position.

He had left a message with Quinsey's secretary that he had gone to Golden to interview a possible witness—a flat lie but he wanted to throw smell off the hospital—and had gotten out of the station nearly as soon as the couple, past Quinsey's office when nobody was looking.

What he had really wanted was a beer to settle the hangover but he decided against it and gone to a Wendy's. A burger and fries and shake. Something he hoped his stomach would hold down. He meant to see the six o'clock news but missed it. It was getting close to seven. He finished the hamburger and drank the rest of the malt, fought to hold it down, won the fight and pulled into the hospital parking lot.

It was, of course, full but he took a place reserved for a doctor and made his way into the hospital and up the second floor where they kept the longer term intensive care patients.

She was still there, the respirator pumping her lungs. Nobody was guarding her because neither he nor Dave had requested it, but there were nurses and doctors moving back and forth past the glass cubicle where she lay. She had not been identified yet or there would have been next of kin in evidence. If she had any. A surprising number of people died without identity or next of kin available and were buried as John or Jane Does. A lot of young hookers, he thought, looking down at her body. There were no tracks in her arms and her body didn't look dissipated or covered with the sores that many of them had so it was a good bet she wasn't a hooker and might have next of kin show up.

Dave would work with the Jefferson county authorities on getting an ID; start the machinery, get the prints from her body, medical examination if the prints didn't help. He liked doing that stuff, the paper work, what Push called the numbers shit.

Push hated it. He also hated stakeouts. Back when he worked vice it was the worst part of the job, the goddam stakeouts. They were always sitting on their asses somewhere waiting for somebody to do something and Push had little patience for it. He knew cops that loved it, wanted nothing more than to sit in a car or a funky motel room and watch an intersection or front of a convenience store or bar.

But he hated it.

Inside half an hour at the hospital he was bored numb. He had memorized all the nurses—four of them good looking, two of them not so good looking and one, he decided the best nurse, almost ugly. He had memorized the interns—all pale and thin from working too many hours and eating slop food and never getting into the daylight—and two orderlies who worked the floor. The doctor who had helped them had gone off duty but had apparently left word as to what they were doing because after an hour a nurse's aide brought him a cup of coffee.

She was young and had dirty blonde hair and slate blue eyes, like Paul Newman, and a straight back and carriage that made Push feel old. She surprised him by being a cop buff—somebody interested in cop work almost to the point of obsession. Usually somebody who has no knowledge of how boring most of it is.

"It must be exciting," she said, half flirting. "Waiting like this on a stakeout."

Hell, Push thought, if a nurse's aide knows then it must be all over the hospital. The essence, he thought, of a good stakeout is secrecy. Well done.

"Not very," he said. "Most of it is boring . . ."

And of course she thought he was just being modest and so she flirted harder. The old John Wayne thing. Go on without me, these arrows don't hurt—why no ma'am, we aren't excited or afraid, danger is our business. He knew officers who took advantage of the situation and kept a string of feminine buffs on the line, told them the most godawful cops stories—all bullshit—but he never could do it without feeling like he was somehow lying to children. They wanted so much to believe what they saw on television or read in books and it was all so much crap. If you told them the truth about it, about the boredom or the dreams or the busted marriages or how many cops eat their guns, they didn't hear it because they didn't want to believe it was that way.

Nine o'clock came and went and still Dave had not arrived nor had he called. Night things started to happen. Two men were brought in downstairs to intensive care with knife wounds. One of them was treated and released with defense wounds on his arms. The other was more serious. The knife had gone low in his chest and nicked an intestine and let the intestine contents out into the body cavity. This would, ultimately, cause an infection that would bring on peretonitis and kill him—it would take weeks before the crime became murder—but in the meantime he had to stay in intensive care for longer term treatment so they brought him up after he was worked on below.

A cop came in with the dying man but Push didn't know him—he seemed to know fewer and fewer of the younger men and women on the force—so he didn't speak to him. The patrol officer left shortly and Push went back to his vigil.

Ten o'clock.

The buff had come three times with coffee and he thanked her each time but cut the conversation off so she'd leave and do bedpans, or whatever a nurse's aide did.

This, he thought, was insane. There was no chance this bastard would come to the hospital. They were just grabbing at air. He went to a phone to call Rosa. He missed her always, and when he thought of her directly the missing could become almost too intense—especially if he were sick, bored or both. As he was now with the hangover and stakeout. He never knew when her husband would be on a flight so they had worked a code if he was there. This time she did not use the code but couldn't talk long because he was only temporarily gone and was out on business but would be home soon.

"We went to a party earlier and just got home a bit ago if you tried to call before—a friend was promoted and we went to celebrate . . ." She trailed off.

"I wondered when you could get away again."

"I thought we decided not to do this anymore."

"You decided. I miss you—miss the hell out of you."

Silence. Then she sighed. "He flies later in the week I think. I'll call you."

They hung up. At ten to eleven Dave finally came in. He looked tired and strung out.

"Jefferson County is blowing up," he said, sipping some of the coffee Push handed him. "Everybody is blaming everybody else for handling it all wrong . . ."

Push nodded. "Anything that will help?"

Dave shook his head. "Nothing. Blood all over the goddam place but we figured that. No usable tracks. Jesus, kids with four-wheelers have been through since this afternoon. Can you believe that? The little shits tore it all apart. Might as well sell tickets and get tourists involved." He leaned back in the chair and stretched. "I'm wrecked. I feel like I've been welded to a car. Anything shaking here?"

Push shook his head. "I think this is a bust."

"Let's give it a little longer. We've got this much in it and we're going to get our ass chewed for it anyway. We might as well ride it out."

"Agreed."

"What's the setup?"

They were sitting in an alcove directly across the hall from the glass cubicle that held the girl. They were hidden to both sides so anybody coming into the hall to approach the cubicle would not see them.

"It's good for one here but awful tight for two," Dave said. "Awful close to the subject too. Why don't I check out the stairs and watch there. It figures he won't use the elevator. The stairs are more private."

"If he comes."

"If he comes."

Dave moved off down the hall to the stairway door and Push went back to waiting. He watched the respirator moving the girl's chest and knew that it supplied air to lungs that kept the heart beating somehow. She was dead but he wondered for the hundredth time or more if she really was dead. If the lungs kept air coming in and oxygen flowing to the brain couldn't she be alive technically, and just not be showing it?

Stupid questions. He used them to keep awake. Like if you shot a man known to have AIDS who was threatening to bite you, would a plea of self-defense stand up in a court of law? Anything to keep awake.

Midnight came and with it the shift change. A new crop of nurses got off the elevator and he studied them as they moved to the center desk to get briefed by the nurses leaving. Uniforms fresh and clean and unwrinkled. Young. They all looked young to him. They had assumed the cutter was a man but they had no evidence to support that. What if it was a woman? What if it was one of the nurses? Right, he thought. What if it was one of the nurses and she had AIDS and threatened to bite him and he had to shoot her . . .

The sound was alien to the floor.

Some part of his brain—he called it the cop part—had registered all the sounds and sights and movements of the floor, of the area. The hum of equipment, the movement of people in their soft-soled shoes, the rustle of paper on charts, the low talk of the nurses and female doctors and the occasional masculine sound of a male orderly or doctor.

There was, suddenly, a new and strange sound in the background.

It was a heavy sound. It came from the left and he thought of it as thump but it was more prolonged. Two or three thumps so close together they were almost a heavy brushing. Something rolling or sliding down. Left was the direction of the stairwell. Dave was in the stairwell.

Push was out and moving without thinking. The snubnose revolver was in his hand automatically, held down and at an angle.

Pictures frozen in his brain. Nurses at the desk recoiling at the sudden appearance of a man with a gun. One raising her hand in protest. Then he was by them and at the door to the stairwell.

He looked quickly through the small window covered with mesh high in the center of the door and ducked back.

Nothing.

He held the gun out in front with both hands, slammed the release bar of the door with his hip and rolled in and left, the gun ready to fire.

Near him, at the door, there was nothing. Below him on the landing half a flight down where the stairs curved to the left and went down again there was some small movement and he moved the revolver to cover the movement, saw it was a leg with the foot wiggling slightly, the toe rubbing, saw at the same instant it was Dave's leg.

Far below, at the bottom, a door slammed.

"Dave?"

There was a sharp gulping sound, followed by another.

"Dave?"

He dropped the handgun to his side and took the six steps down to the landing in two bounds.

"Dave?"

He was lying face down, his head and face over the top step of the next flight starting down. His toe kept rubbing, pushing, and one of his hands was back and palm up with the fingers closing and unclosing.

"*Dave?*"

Push turned without kneeling and screamed. "Doctor! Nurse! Anybody—down here now. In the stairwell. *Now!*"

He kneeled next to Dave, tried to find the wound, talking it down. "Easy now, easy. You'll be all right. They're coming. Right here. They'll be right here."

And they did come fast. Two nurses slammed through the door like football players, took one look, called back for two orderlies with a folding gurney table who were there in seconds followed by a doctor. Push jacked back out of the way as they rolled Dave over.

His eyes were open but flat. His coat had opened and in the center of his shirt, almost in the middle of his chest, there was a small spot of blood.

They had him on the gurney, two holding and two lifting as they carried him back up to the floor and directly into intensive care next to the body of the girl. He was too tall for the table and his feet hung over the end. All in rehearsed, practiced motions. They cut his shirt open, found the wound. A slot in his body. A small slot just beneath the sternum.

Talk. They talked. Push heard their talk. All technical terms about the wound, what to plug in, what to clean away. Tubes down his throat. Respirator. Machines. They hit him with two massive injections, trying to stimulate the heart, then brought out the two "paddles" and jolted him electrically once, again, again and again and, finally, the doctor turned to Push. Shook his head.

"Dave?" he said. "But it was all right. He was moving. We're in a hospital. Do something."

"His heart is damaged. He was stabbed and the knife actually penetrated the bottom of the heart. It won't come back—there is nothing to do."

"Do something, goddamit." He grabbed the doctor's tunic, pulled him forward. "Do something more now!"

The doctor waited, said nothing. He had done this many times. He had read papers on how to handle this. Death was part of what he did. He had actually taken a class on how to handle this.

Push shook his head. "See, we were just talking a bit ago . . ."

The doctor signaled one of the nurses who came forward and took Push by the elbow. Push followed her out into the hall. Then he stopped and turned back.

"Fix his feet. They hang over the table. Fix them now. Put something under them. Please put something under them."

Oh, he thought. He was standing facing the wall. Some kind of chart with veins in it. Oh. He's dead. Oh. Dave is dead. Dave Thorsen is dead. Dave Thorsen my partner is dead. Dave Thorsen my partner is dead and I didn't do anything to help him.

Oh.

Oh no.

Then he remembered the sound of the closing door below when he was with Dave on the landing. That had been him. That had been the cutter leaving. He ran to the stairwell and slammed the door open, ran as if he could catch him, ran as if the trail were still warm.

Ran as if it mattered.

CHAPTER
THIRTEEN

Quinsey was furious. No, more than that—enraged to a point of insanity. Spit frothed at the corners of his mouth and the cords in his neck were swollen with it, pumping his face red, jerking his shoulders into a hunch as he stood in back of his desk with both hands clenched into knotted fists that he kept slamming down into the top of the desk as he spoke. His voice sounded like breaking glass.

Push stared out the large glass window at the squad room, ignored the lieutenant, which did nothing but infuriate him more. Men and women worked at their desks but Push knew it was all for show. The squad room was a theater and they were all an audience, watching him, waiting for him, waiting for Quinsey to nail him.

"I'm sorry about Thorsen," Quinsey was saying. "But the two of you have done everything as backwards as you could on this investigation. Has it occurred to you that if you had done the right thing Thorsen would still be alive?"

Push had taken care of all the partner work that went with sudden death. He had spoken to Dave's wife, held her while she cried; he had spoken to the stewardess, held her while she cried. He had cleaned Dave's locker, making sure there was no porno or a hideout gun or other embarrassing material—there wasn't—before turning it over to the widow. That's how it was written in the unwritten manuals. Turning it over to the widow. The Widow.

Shit.

He had done it all without breaking down, all without emotion showing. The rock. He'd done it because he was supposed to do it. Took a whole day to do it. There would be a small service—no elaborate line-of-duty stuff for Dave. He wouldn't have wanted it. Just Push and the family and then a cremation and an urn. The funeral was later today. Two days after the death. One day Dave had been worried about impotence, couldn't get it up, and two days later he was ashes.

Ahh, he thought, ahhh shit.

He had gone to the autopsy. He had to know what kind of knife killed Dave. But he could not bring himself to go into the cutting room and had waited outside for the information. Partners, he thought—even partners that didn't work together all the time—police partners were closer than family. Closer than skin. He could not believe the pain. The thing ripped at him.

"You could have had backup, could have had support . . ."

Of course all this was just Quinsey covering his ass.

Push knew that. If they had told the lieutenant about the stakeout he would not have allowed it because it was the wrong setup; improper procedure. And Quinsey was far too chickenshit to have taken a chance on it.

"If you'd followed correct procedure none of this would have had to happen."

Push turned from the window and looked at the lieutenant. There was nothing this son of a bitch could say about him, could say to him, that he had not already thought of himself. They did not make words bad enough, thoughts bad enough to match what had happened at night for the last two nights. He had replayed every single moment of what had happened—opening the stairwell door, seeing Dave lying there, the sound of the slamming door down at the bottom of the staircase, Dave's toe pushing at the floor, Dave's hand opening and closing, the gulping sounds as he tried to get air, the open flat look in his eyes when they rolled him over, the small slot in his chest just below the sternum—replayed it again and again through the night, through each day.

Now. While Quinsey prattled on and on he replayed it.

The death of Dave. His own little private theater of horror, always ready for instant replay in his brain, goaded by the question: What if? What if I had done the stairwell and left Dave in the alcove? What if I had reacted to the sound a second sooner? What if I had really believed in the stakeout? What if I had never been born?

Two nights without sleep. Eyes open, driving in the

car, hating, hating all things. Hating the cutter and the night and the world but most, most of all, hating himself. He'd tried bed the second night but could only stand it for a second after he closed his eyes and all of it came rushing in. He'd gotten up, gotten dressed and spent the whole night in a Denny's drinking coffee and going to the can every ten minutes.

"You are off the case," Quinsey said. "As of now. Off the case and off work. You are suspended until I can figure out what to do with you. Give me your gun and badge." He held out his hand.

"Eat shit." It was the first thing Push had said since coming into Quinsey's office.

"What?"

"I said eat shit. You can take me off the case or leave me on. It doesn't matter because I'll get the bastard anyway and you won't stop me because I know about your honey out on Colfax. I also know you get suits at Lapere's for nothing." God how he hated Quinsey.

"You son of a bitch. Where do you get off spying on me?"

Push didn't answer the question, instead asked one. "Does that mean I'm not suspended?"

"Get the hell out of my office!"

"Thank you. I knew you'd see it my way." Push left the office. In the squad room nobody spoke but there were some smiles. He was surrounded by a protective wall, almost a barrier of grief that nobody would try to penetrate. They knew him and knew Dave and knew how close the two of them had been and they respected that.

They might step up and say what a bummer it was, Dave being gone, or say a small word about how they'd miss him—speaking to Push as if he'd lost a loved one, a close family member, which, indeed he had—but they rapidly moved away, left him alone with it.

And he wanted to be alone.

He wanted to be alone and work alone and track the son of a bitch alone. No part of what he intended to do had anything to do with correct police procedure and if he went down he wanted to go down alone.

He stopped at Cartier's desk and left a brief note telling him they'd have to put a hold on setting up the Juniper arrest. Tracking down the cutter was now all there was, all he would do.

He called the medical examiner's office. They were going to collate the information about the wounds that killed Betti Fencer and the wounds that killed the unknown girl and the wound that killed Dave and see if there was any further information they could give him. Other than that it looked to be the same size and length of knife they had nothing new for him and he'd known that from the autopsy. The blow from the knife had come from below and up, probably with some force, not just a poke but a lifting, stabbing motion with some weight in back of it.

Whoever did it was close, right next to Dave, and the fact that Dave had not pulled his revolver indicated that it was a complete surprise. The night it happened Push had run down the stairs and out the door in a kind of focused panic, almost an attack against time, trying to catch the cutter though he knew it was impossible. In the parking lot he saw nothing moving, stood with his gun in his hand, sucking air, sobbing until he could control himself. Then he had gone back into the hospital. Two receptionists at the front desk told him that a doctor in a pale blue doctor's tunic had run through the lobby and out the door. They had not seen him well enough to identify him. He had dark hair and was wearing sunglasses. Tall, well-built, carrying something in a towel. That's all they remembered.

He thanked the medical examiner's office and hung up. They had added that they would later today run a Jane Doe autopsy on the girl from the hospital. It was scheduled for afternoon. No next of kin had turned up yet and there hadn't been a print match in any national or state record for ID so the hospital had gotten a court order to pull the plug and she was now in the morgue.

How did it scan, he thought—Dave's death—as he walked out of the squad room and down to the parking lot to drive to Dave's funeral service. How did Dave's death happen? He tried to be objective, fought to keep his emotions down—as if it were any homicide. How did the crime scene work? Somebody coming up the stairs, somebody dressed as a doctor, which threw Dave off, and when he got close to Dave he suddenly knifed him. No. That didn't work.

There had to be some surprise to it somehow. If Dave had seen somebody coming up the stairs, carrying a towel and wearing shades, doctor's uniform or not he would have been suspicious, would have had his gun out or at least scuffled. Yelled before he got stabbed.

Unless Dave didn't see him.

There.

That fit. If Dave didn't see him . . . but how could that be? Push stopped with his hand on the car door handle, stared across the parking lot, trying to think of that night. Why wouldn't Dave be ready for him?

Dave was asleep. He had been at the crime scene up by Evergreen all day and had then driven back down to the city to meet Push at the hospital. He'd even mentioned being tired.

That was it. He'd settled on a step in the stairwell and gone to sleep and the cutter had come up around a corner and there Dave was, just sitting there, waiting for him. Sleeping. Perhaps Dave had moved and startled or surprised the cutter and the cutter reached up—that would explain the angle of the entry wound as well—and shoved the knife in.

Push stiffened with it, with the feeling of it—could sense the knife going in, up and in. Jesus, Dave—oh Jesus I'm sorry.

He shook. Not just his head but shook all over, a chill that turned into a tremor he couldn't stop until he'd bitten his tongue and slammed his fist into the top of the car.

He got in and turned the key and as soon as the radio came on there was a message for him.

"Call the missing persons number on a groundline—they have an ID on your Jane Doe from the hospital."

Push turned off the car and ran back into the station.

162

CHAPTER
FOURTEEN

It was hard to believe the woman in missing persons was a police officer. She looked to be about nineteen and a cheerleader, with what Dave would have called a "twixey" little body that jiggled a lot and was hard not to stare at. Her blonde hair was cut evenly all around, with straight bangs, and she had enormous blue eyes with long lashes and an innocent, completely beguiling look. Even her name was straight cheerleader—Kerri Anderson.

But she had attended the academy and had graduated in the top ten percent of her class—had qualified expert with her revolver and had a black belt in karate—and worked a time in traffic before this transfer to missing persons. The kid patrol. Most of missing persons work was trying to find kids, some of them almost as old as this officer Push now stood next to, waiting.

"We got a call from a woman at a singles place in Westwood," she was saying, ignoring Push's impatience. "Her roommate was missing. We get about a thousand of those a week I think. Along with teenage girls missing and almost none of them are really missing. But this time something hit me. The roommate said she worked at the airport and hadn't shown up for work and I've heard all the rumors about this cutter you're working. So I put two and two together . . ."

"You did this all on your own?" Push asked the question as a courtesy. He really wanted to scream at her to finish but everybody, he knew, everybody needed strokes.

"It was nothing, really. She worked at Federal Rental—a car rental. So I called them and they told me she had been there a year and a half without an unexplained absence—you always check that first, to see if they're floaters or not, unsteady in their habits—and then they told me she'd had to do a minimum security clearance to get the job because it's at the airport."

"Prints," Push cut in. "You got prints."

She nodded, smiling. "They sent them over by courier—were really cooperative. And I compared them. It's a dead bang match. Every finger and one thumb are perfect. The other thumb had a cut on it."

Push waited.

"Her name is Linda Raimey." Kerri picked up a sheet of paper and read from it. "As I said she works at Federal Car Rental at the airport, lives at 2941 Elm in Westwood, is twenty-two years old—was twenty-two years old—not married, never been, and no children."

Push took the paper. The airport. It was at the airport—the goddam place kept coming up. The answer was there. "Thank you. For all this, the extra work—you did good."

"I heard about your partner," she said as Push turned to go. "Kick the bastard's ass . . ."

Push was out the door before he could hear the rest of the sentence.

In the hall he used a pay phone and called the lab, asked them about prints in the hospital. It was a shot in the dark and this time it didn't pay off. They had checked the whole stairwell area, the handrails and walls, and had several hundred different prints but no way to compare them to anybody. So many people had gone up and down the stairs . . . but they'd keep all the prints on record in case they could be used to corroborate later.

Push thanked Melon. Now, he thought, now I am using courtesy and good investigative procedures—now that Dave is gone and everything is in pieces—now I am working right.

He dropped another quarter in the phone and called the Jefferson County people who handled the two crime scenes in the mountains. They had nothing new to report except a possible—only possible—link with some evidence.

"What evidence?" Push asked. He watched two cops coming in the door, saw them recognize him, saw the pity in their eyes.

"Some tubers riding innertubes down the creek that runs by the cutoff found a rubber glove a mile and a half downstream from the crime scene, stuck in some rocks. They called us and we've got the glove and now have people searching for another one but it would be a miracle if we found it." The sheriff's deputy paused. "I'm not sure if we can do justice to the glove—handle it right. I want to turn it over to you if that's possible."

A hunch triggered and Push nodded, as if the deputy could see him. "Good thinking. Take it to the lab downtown—if you can—and tell them to compare any prints they get from inside the glove to the prints from the hospital wall . . . Never mind, I'll call them on it."

He signed off, dug out another quarter and called the lab again and told Melon about the glove and comparing anything to the hospital wall. Rubber gloves were usually good for prints on the inside.

"Except for the water," the Melon said. "If the water got inside the glove and sloshed around it might have ruined the prints . . ."

"Shoot for it anyway," Push said. "I'll be moving all day" (and from now on, he thought) "so I'll call in later from time to time."

"Am I authorized to go overtime on this?" Melon asked.

Push thought. If he said yes the whole thing would have to be cleared through Quinsey, who would flat not help. "No. I can't authorize it on this—he won't clear it." They both knew who "he" was. "But as a favor . . ." He let it hang there.

"I know it's about Thorsen," he said, "and it's no problem with me working overtime. I'll do it. But I can't make the techs stay without some authorization."

"I understand."

"I'll work alone if nobody will stay with me. But it might take a little longer. There were a hell of a lot of prints from that hospital and to compare them one by one could take all night."

"Thanks. I owe you on this."

"No sweat."

Push hung the mike back in the bracket and looked at his watch. The funeral service was in half an hour. He'd do that and then go to the airport.

He pushed the accelerator down. Things were happening now. There was movement.

Dave, he thought again—it was always there—Dave liked this part of an investigation best. When it started to quicken, move, started to shake loose. Dave would have liked this . . .

Interiors
Five

They came to him in the night this time.

All swirling in bright colored feathers and huge head-dresses, hair matted with blood, the ancient ones, the gods came in the night in a dream. They were in a row, facing him with their painted and scarred faces and he thought at first they were angry. They were silent and huge and covered in smears and handprints of blood and he felt small, humble. Then one of them, in a deep voice, told him it was all right. He had done the right thing.

For days he had worried that he had done it wrong and they would be angry with him. He had killed the man at the hospital almost by accident, coming around the corner and almost stumbling on him asleep that way. He had just pushed with the knife, almost as if pushing with his hand, and the knife had gone up and in by itself and when the man fell-lunged forward against the blade his coat had opened and he had seen the gun and known he was the police and had run.

That was what he thought he had done wrong. To run that way and leave the girl alive. If she identified him the police would stop him and destroy his work. But when the day passed and another and then they announced on the news that she had died and the policeman was dead as well—when all that happened and the police had not come for him he knew he was safe.

And that night they came to him while he was sleeping and told him he was good, that he had done the right thing. It awakened him, the good feeling they gave him, and he sat in the dark thinking of it—he had been so worried about angering them—and he knew that they wanted him to do it again.

Now.

He could not say why he knew it but the feeling was strong, stronger than it had ever been—they wanted him to find another one and they wanted him to do it as soon as he could.

He got out of bed and went into the study where he had the Aztec artifacts. He touched a stone carving he had stolen from one of the temples on one of his trips to Mexico. It was the picture of deity, carved in bas relief, and even in the small carving the deity looked great and terrible with all the power of the gods in his visage.

He wore only his shorts and sat in the leather chair at his desk, curled in a ball, hugging his knees and not feeling the cold leather on his bare back, and studied the rest of the carvings in the glass case. The stone gods. He did not discover them, discover the Aztecs and know why he did what he did, until after the first woman, the first ritual. That was back in Cleveland, the first time—he smiled now remembering how crude it had been, not a true ritual at all, no beauty to it—and then he had gone to Mexico on a vacation with his wife and learned of the Aztec sacrifices when visiting their temples. He had known then that the Aztecs knew, that they had known for centuries—ripping the beating hearts out of the chosen—and so he bought and stole images of their gods. He had them in stone and concrete all around his house and out by the pool. People commented on them and told him how beautiful the statues were and he would smile and nod. But he knew more than they did, more than anybody did about the Aztecs, about the Aztec gods. He knew why they had to do what they did, why they sacrificed.

Why they must be horrible and beautiful at the same time. If there were not sacrifices, if there were not rituals it would all end; if the gods were not appeased and shown correctly that they were honored they would stop everything, end everything.

They, the gods, could not be without this belief; could not exist unless it were proven to them again and again. They needed him—and he supposed there must be others like him, others who knew—just as he needed them They needed him to do the ritual.

And they wanted it now. They did not say it in the dream but they did not have to say it. He knew what they wanted, could feel it in their terrible stares and knew that he could not rest. They wanted another now and he thought it must be because the last one didn't count. There had to be another one soon to make up for it.

But he would have to be careful. He had been lucky last time, very lucky. He could not do another one in this area. It would have to be away. Far enough away to avoid suspicion.

He had a trip coming in two days. He was flying to Seattle on a late flight with a one day layover while they serviced the 727 at Boeing. That would be it. He could do it in Seattle. He would go to Seattle and see if they came to him and told him to do it; came to him and showed him the one they wanted. That would be far enough away.

Yes. They could come to him in Seattle. Yes.

His wife came into the study, walked up in back of him and stood with her hands on his cheeks, holding his head, and asked if anything was wrong and he said no, nothing was wrong, and pushed his head back between her breasts. They felt warm and soft.

You haven't been awakened at night for a long time, she told him, real concern in her voice—is it the bad dreams again? The dreams about your mother? And he said no, he was just concerned about an upcoming flight test. It wasn't that important, but he kept thinking about it and couldn't sleep, and she leaned forward and ran her hands down on him and he became hard and they went back together, holding hands, and made love until they were both tired and she slept.

But he opened his eyes as soon as her breathing became regular and thought: I hear you, it's all right.

I hear you.

CHAPTER
FIFTEEN

The manager of Federal Car Rental proved to be as cooperative as Kerri had said. After the funeral service—a sad, tired little thing that didn't match Dave at all—Push had driven to the airport and found him in an office in back of the rental booths. He was young, Push was convinced that everybody was young, with short hair and a well-fitted suit with a vest, and looked straightforward and tough in some way—in his eyes—and he had a small mustache and even brown eyes. His name was John Warren.

"I hired Linda personally," he said. "Anything I can do to help—you just say the word."

What the hell, Push thought, might as well give it a shot. "Could I get a list of the rentals she made on her last day at work?"

The manager hesitated, thinking. "We have a problem with that . . ."

There went cooperation, Push thought, but he was wrong.

"She worked eight-hour shifts and we run a fifteen-hour day, plus it's arranged in weeks and not days, for accounting purposes. We'll have to go back through and work the list and times against her hours to be exact and to get all the rentals with her name on them."

"If I get the list I could do the same thing."

"Sure." He nodded. "But you don't know the system and it would take you a full day. I'll have my office do it in an hour. Can you wait an hour?"

Push nodded, not believing how nice the man was being. An old cop adage said never to take an apple when you could get the whole store. Might as well keep trying. "Could I interview the people who worked with her?"

Another quick nod. "You're in luck. This would have been her shift and the girl she worked with is out there now. I'll bring her in."

"Would it be possible for me to interview her alone?"

"No problem. I'll take her place while she's in here. Better yet I'll go upstairs to the main office and get those rental records for you."

He went through the door and in a moment a girl came in. She was pert, lively looking—a brunette with hair cut so it fell evenly all around about chin level. She looked scared but her voice was steady. "I'm Peggy Finley. I worked with Linda before this . . . terrible thing happened. Mr. Warren said you wanted to ask me some questions."

Push nodded, motioned her to sit down at Warren's desk. "Relax. I just need some general information about Linda, if you don't mind."

She sat and Push settled himself on the corner of the

desk, the way Dave liked to do. "Let's start with anything you think might be of interest to me about the last day she worked."

Peggy frowned, thinking. "That was Monday, I think. We came in at six in the morning and worked until two that day. Monday is a heavy car day because a lot of people bring them back from the weekends and there are some who want to rent for the week—commuters who come in Sunday night and need a car all week—so we're pretty busy in the morning. I worked one side of the booth and she worked the other and for five or six hours we kept so busy we hardly said a word to each other."

"Do you remember any of her customers—renters?"

Peggy thought a moment, then shook her head. "It was so busy that it was all I could do to keep up. I don't even remember most of the people I rented cars to. We have this big promotional campaign on—this ten dollar a day thing?—and you wouldn't believe the crowds we get. No, I don't remember her customers at all. Just the bit about her date."

Push had been going to let her go. He stopped now, his hand half up. "What about a date?"

"When the rush was over we had a cup of coffee. We're not supposed to eat or drink while we're working so don't tell Mr. Warren. But when there's such a rush you can't get coffee and when you come to work at six in the morning and don't get coffee . . ."

The date, Push wanted to scream, get to the fucking date. He smiled. Kept his mouth shut.

". . . so we had some coffee and I think Linda had a

roll too. We had about ten minutes and she went for coffee and when she came back I could see she was pleased about something. She smiles a funny way—I mean smiled, don't I? She had this way of smiling when she was happy, like a cartoon cat that just got a bird. She had this smile and I asked her what it was about and she said she had gotten a date and that he was an eight."

"What did eight mean?"

Peggy smiled and Push thought it was probably like the smile she had described for Linda. "Ten is the best and one is a real mouthbreather—a slump. You never date anything under a five and you never meet a ten unless he's already married. That's Murphy's Law. And you're always looking to move up. Since a ten is impossible the best is nine, and an eight is very, very high. I thought she was kidding, but she wasn't. He was a definite eight."

"How do you know that?"

"Well, it's complicated. I've only dated one eight in my life and that was a doctor who wasn't gay, had never been married and was not—you know—sick. It didn't work out, but that's life. And I knew a lawyer once who I think was an eight but I never dated him because my roommate was after him. It's money, part of it, but not just that—money and looks and the way a man moves and even his buns."

"His buns?"

"Yes." She laughed now, even white teeth flashing. "A man should have tight, round buns, no gut, a clean appearance, good shoulders and lots of money."

I'm about a three, Push thought—maybe a four. My buns are all right. But that's it.

"And the way she described this date he had it all. Plus the money," she continued.

"What did she say about the money?"

"Nothing really direct. But she knew his job and it's a money job . . ."

"What was his job?" Push could smell it now. The way a wolf smells blood and moves in.

"He was a pilot."

Bingo. "Did you know him—did she say his name?" Please, he thought now, please god please god please god . . .

Peggy thought, chewing a perfect lower lip with perfect caps. "No. He came in and rented a car and must have waited for her to go to coffee to ask her out because I don't remember seeing him at the booth. I mean you can see how busy it was—for me to miss seeing an eight that way. She did say he wasn't wearing a ring and didn't show a white circle on his finger. We look for that right away, especially on the good ones. And he wasn't."

"Anything else at all—anything about the way he looked? Anything."

"No . . . just that he was a pilot and of course he must have been good looking and not too old or anything like that for her to call him an eight. Old ones are never eights."

I'm a three, he thought—definite three with good buns maybe.

"Does all this help?"

He nodded, hiding his elation. "It all helps."

Just then there was a tap on the office door and Warren looked in. "If you're close to done we have some lines starting out here."

Peggy got up and Push thanked her as she left to return to work.

"Any help at all?" Warren asked, coming into the office.

"Some, I think." Rule six, he thought, always act pessimistic. You'll get more. Besides, as Dave used to say, if you're a pessimist you're right most of the time. He had said it at least once a day.

"Here's the list. It had been entered into the computer so I had them lock in the time and date from Linda's last shift and then had them run a printout—it went much faster than I thought it would. There's no printout with all the rental agreements, addresses and information on it, and I had them run another print with just names and addresses. I thought that might make it quicker."

Push took the long, folded sheets of the printout covered with pale green and white bars. "You've been more than helpful—I just wish everybody was this easy to work with."

Warren moved to the back of his desk. "This is an awful thing. I understand she was stabbed repeatedly. Horrible. Just catch the bastard . . ."

Push was out of the office and riding up the escalator to reach the main floor before he looked at the list. The printout had come unfolded in his hand and started to drop and when he picked it up he almost idly scanned the

list of names and information. He didn't expect anything—names and dates and cars. It would take hours to
go over it, then somehow find out which ones were pilots.
He was thinking that he could perhaps get the insurance
companies for the unions to cross-reference the list somehow, to tell him if any of them were pilots, when his eyes
hit the name.

The fourth name on the list riveted him, stopped his
breath and his thinking so that he forgot he was on an
escalator and almost tripped when he came to the top.
The lady in back of him swore and stepped around him.

Stephen Baylor.

Rosa, he thought. Rosa's name was Baylor and her
husband was named Stephen.

And he was a pilot.

CHAPTER SIXTEEN

Courts allowed many things in their rush to free the guilty, Packard used to tell Push. In the interests of protecting the civil rights of the accused and ignoring those of the victim, they stretched truth and logic so fine you could see through it; and the one thing they screwed up on the worst, he would say—belching the silent beer belches that sounded like farts smelled in the patrol car— was to allow the most insane set of coincidental happenings to go by because they were viewed only as circumstantial evidence and couldn't be strictly proven.

One of the many Packard rules that Push agreed with was that coincidences simply didn't happen. The odds, Packard stated, the sheer mathematical odds against it were so overwhelming as not to exist. That was the real world. The problem was that the courts didn't exist in the real world, the street world, the world where women get breasts cut off. The courts existed in a lofty, silly and unrealistic world where crime never happened but was only discussed. In the real world crime was almost never discussed and happened all the time.

The police, Packard believed and said often, were in that thin line where the real world began and the court world met and they had to bring the two together and since it was an impossible job—they couldn't truly exist together because they were so different—the police could never succeed, must always, inevitably fail. Evidence gathered as a result of coincidence, a guess or because a cop just "thought a perpetrator looked hinky," would not be allowed even if the suspect was guilty as hell, dripped with blood and admitted to the crime.

And here he was, Push thought, mashing the accelerator to the floor and boring the unmarked car up I-70 through the outskirts of Denver heading for Evergreen— here he was with an impossible coincidence.

He needed a pilot.

He had one.

He needed a pilot who had rented a car at a given time and date from Linda Raimey.

He had one.

He needed a pilot who was not accounted for on the night Dave was killed.

He had one. Rosa had said her husband was out, not on a flight but out on business the night Dave was killed. Sure, Push thought, the asshole was on his way down to the hospital.

It all fit. Not just one, two, but three coincidences. The odds against one were farfetched. Two were staggering. Three were impossible. And what had Rosa said: he had been acting moody, withdrawn, when he came off of trips. Baylor had to be the one.

Yet if he played it the "right" way he should get a warrant—would have to show probable cause why he should get a warrant—and no judge would do it based on simple coincidence. There had to be evidence. If he played it straight he couldn't make a bust, couldn't get his hands on the bastard, couldn't tear him down. Couldn't rip him and tear him down and get . . .

And there was Rosa. Who knew when Baylor would trigger and start cutting her up? He was crazy, completely whacky—anything could set him off. Push had seen whackos go so nuts they started to cut themselves up, eat their own hands. Push was certain she didn't know about him. It would have come out—in her manner if nothing else. So she was living with a time bomb and didn't know it.

He jammed his foot down harder just as the car started up the Lookout Mountain section of the freeway, heading for Genesee Pass. It did not speed up noticeably but he kept it mashed down, leaning forward.

At El Rancho restaurant he'd have to turn off, then go through Bergen Park to the outskirts of Evergreen where they lived in a rich development. He knew her address—2340 Parrot Way—but had no idea where it was and he couldn't use the Jefferson County people because he was going in without a warrant and they wouldn't support him.

He roared over Genesee Pass, started the downhill run to the Bergen Park-Evergreen turnoff at El Rancho, and quickly pegged the speedometer. The car, a fairly new Dodge with the big engine, acted like a hundred and twenty was cruising speed and he virtually floated to the exit. He took it, ran the stop at the bottom and wound through mountain roads for four miles with the Dodge lifting gently on the corners.

In Bergen Park he slid to a stop in a gas station, asked the man at the glass booth where Parrot Way was located and was given a set of directions that he fought to memorize.

His mind was seething, roaring with all of it now. He saw Dave again, the little cut in his chest, the little killing cut and his hands moving and his flat eyes; it mixed with Rosa moving on top of him in the motel rooms and the sudden appearance of a cut in her chest, a small cut, a killing cut between her breasts and all of it, all of it mixed with fear, core fear, soul fear.

Parrot Way was a hidden road, a cut-back off the highway, and he almost missed the sign. Just as he passed he saw it, braked hard, backed up with smoke curling off the tires, slammed the Dodge into drive and floored it around the corner.

The houses were not on the street itself but set back in wooded driveways. He saw a wooden mailbox with 2340 carved into its side, under the gouged words THE BAYLORS, and he whipped the Dodge so hard it fishtailed and hit the mailbox with the left rear fender, knocking it over. He floored it again, only to find the driveway short, and just as the Dodge leaped forward he found himself looking head on into twin garage doors. Almost too late he jammed his foot on the brake and brought the nose around and the car slid sideways to a stop in a great screeching of tires.

He was out of the car and moving to the front door—oak set in a great expanse of cedar and glass, a money door in a money wall—before the dust had settled.

In the middle of the door was a steel steer head arranged as a knocker and he slammed it twice and when there wasn't an immediate answer he tried the knob.

It wasn't locked. He pulled his revolver, held it in both hands, ready, opened the door with his shoulder and moved in, the gun half up.

The world froze in time. Rosa, wearing blue jeans and a tee shirt, half way across a living room to answer the door, a drink in one hand that she was placing on an end table near a rich, black leather couch, looking up to see—in a mixture of stunned surprise and horror—Push come in the door with a drawn gun, moving low and to the right to not silhouette himself against the light from outside.

And coming from a batwing door obviously leading back into the kitchen a man with a straight build, distinguished dark hair gray at the temples, wearing a loose cashmere sweater. He was holding a long butcher knife with a thick, triangular blade.

The handgun moved by itself. Took the center of mass. Push's fingers started to squeeze. Two pounds, that's all it would take. Two and half pounds and one of the jacketed hollow-point bullets—holdover from vice days—would take out the center of mass. The center of the man's chest.

"Freeze," Push said loudly—loudness helped to

control, to own a situation. "I'm the police. Drop the knife and freeze or I'll blow your fucking head off."

The man—Stephen Baylor—did nothing for half a second and Push started to pull the round off. He didn't care now. Dave, the hacked-up girls, it was all there, and he took off the slack on the trigger. Then the knife fell.

"Push," Rosa said. "Are you out of your goddam mind?"

"You know him?" Stephen asked. As if the question were more important than the fact that a man was standing holding a gun on him.

"You have the right to remain silent," Push said, the gun still holding the center of mass. "Anything you say can and will be used against you . . ."

"Am I under arrest?"

Rosa came forward, started to move between them, but Push moved sideways to keep the path open. "Don't get between us."

"What are you doing here?" she asked, stopping. Her voice was trembling, cracking. "What in hell are you doing here?"

"I'm here to arrest Stephen Baylor in connection with a murder investigation. He is under suspicion in two cases." God, he thought, I sound so formal—what I really want to do is blow this son of a bitch away.

"But that's absurd," Baylor said. "What are you talking about?"

Rosa put her hands to her face, shook her head. "This can't be happening. This just can't be happening."

184

"There is some mistake here," Baylor said. "Some terrible mistake."

"Turn around," Push said, his voice flat. "Now."

Baylor turned and Push cuffed him. Rosa stood all this time in silence, shaking her head, her hands on her cheeks.

Push moved Baylor around, aimed him towards the door, then kicked his legs out from under him and dropped him suddenly on his face. He kneeled in back of him, the gun nestled in the back of his skull. "You will not move—not even breathe."

He turned to Rosa. "Get me a paper sack."

"What?"

"I want a paper sack and all the knives, butcher knives like that one you have on the floor. Take them by the tips of the blades and drop them in the sack and bring them to me."

"But . . . I mean this is all crazy. What's he supposed to have done?"

"Kill. He's supposed to have killed. A woman, several women, then Dave . . ."

"Dave? You mean Dave Thorsen? Is he dead?" She had never met Dave but knew he had been Push's partner and they had spoken about him many times, just as he spoke to Dave about her. "Dave is dead?"

He nodded. "Get the knives."

"I don't understand," Baylor said from the floor to Rosa. "How do you know this man? And how did you know about his partner? What does all this mean?" His voice was muffled in the carpet.

"Get the knives," Push repeated, ignoring Baylor, and to his amazement she nodded and left to find a sack and do as he'd said.

He turned to Baylor, grabbed him by the collar of his sweater and dragged him to his feet. "Up, asshole."

Once up he slammed him with his left hand in the middle of Baylor's back and propelled him out the still-open door. Outside, he opened the rear door of the car and heaved with his forearm and shoulder to mash Baylor in across the seat, face down, rage taking him now, and he kicked at the pilot's legs until they were inside so he could slam the door.

Rosa came out then with a sack full of knives. "Push, this just can't be—Stephen wouldn't do all that. He just wouldn't."

Which of course meant nothing. There was always somebody who said that about everybody who was arrested. "You get the knife on the floor—the one he was holding?"

She nodded. "He was cutting meat for sandwiches . . ." She paused. "He was just cutting some meat for sandwiches and you came in and—oh, Christ, this can't be happening. Is he really under arrest?"

Push nodded, started around the car.

"I mean, you're not just doing this—you know—for us or something?" She looked at him across the roof of the car.

Baylor was still face down in the back seat. The psychological impact of the arrest had him. Street people were used to it, sometimes sat in the back and joked with the cops. But those new to it often suffered a kind of shock and it was not uncommon for them to be speechless, terrified into a numbness. It was also not uncommon for them to go insane and try to tear apart the arresting officer—or officers. Baylor had become quiet and Push put his handgun back in the holster at his right hip.

"He rented a car from a girl who was stabbed with a long knife and left for dead not far from here and it was known that she left after work with a pilot who rented a car from her during the shift before she was killed." He took a deep breath. "We allowed the television news to think she was still alive and they released that information and later that night Dave was attacked and stabbed to death with a long knife about an hour and a half after I called and you said your husband was 'out on business.' It's too close. Then I come for him and he steps out of the kitchen with a long knife in his hand. How does it look to you?"

She was white, her hand to her mouth. "The car— the rental car was for me. There's been a terrible mistake. All of this is a terrible mistake. My car broke down and I told him when he came off his flight that day to rent a car and bring it home to me. He did and I've had it since. I just took it back this morning. He couldn't have done anything because he brought the car straight to me from the airport that morning and we were together the rest of the day. Oh my god."

Push hesitated. His thinking skipped a beat.

"And that night he went to a union meeting. That should be easy to check out."

All this time Baylor had been silent, listening. He rolled over now, rocked and scrambled to a sitting position with his hands awkwardly cuffed to his rear. Cuffed in the rear and sitting in a car means the suspect has to virtually sit on his hands and arms, which throws a warped stress on the shoulders. The shock was leaving Baylor now and was being replaced by anger, rage. He was furious.

"Take the cuffs off," he said through the window. "You've screwed up, like she says. Take them off now, goddamit."

Push studied Rosa's face. Cop thinking dies hard, or never dies at all. She could lie, he thought—could lie for him. She could be lying to save him, making it up as she went. But he knew instinctively that he was wrong. She couldn't be faking the expression, the white lines around her lips, the fear etched in the corners of her eyes.

He'd blown it.

He opened the rear door of the car and helped Baylor out, unlocked the cuffs and put them back on his belt. "I . . . I . . . ." He didn't know what to say, stood there, looking at the two of them.

"Leave," Rosa said, looking directly through him. "Leave now."

"I'll call," he said.

"No." Baylor looked at him, at Rosa, rubbing his wrists. "No you won't. All you'll be doing is hearing from my lawyer. Now get the hell out of here."

Push got in the Dodge and turned around and drove out the driveway and away and back the long drive down into Denver and not once, not once could he think of anything to say.

CHAPTER
SEVENTEEN

There were five pilots who rented cars from Linda during her shift—Baylor was just one of them.

Push had gotten the information, finally, from the credit card companies. He'd had to lie. The insurance company for the pilots' medical insurance and workers compensation benefits—he was grabbing at straws—had slammed the door in his face. But everybody who had paid for a car rental that day had used a credit card and the cards were identified on the rental forms by company so he'd simply called each credit card company, explained that he was with the police working on a credit card scam, given them his badge number and they'd bent over backwards to help him. He went by their offices—there were four different card companies and they were all eager to help—and got the lists. Then he went back to Scarf's because he couldn't work at the station and avoid Quinsey—who was on a rampage—and took a table in back and went to work.

Scarf brought him dark beer and burritos and he compared forms to people to lists until he had identified every person on the list and five of them were pilots.

With Baylor out it left four.

Two of them were women and he knocked them off.

Of the remaining two both were married, had children, lived in the Evergreen area—it seemed to be a hub for pilots—and were about forty. They worked for different airlines but both flew airlines that went to Seattle. One was named Quintara and the other Harvitt and he picked Harvitt first because Quintara sounded Latino or Spanish and one of Packard's rules had been that mostly whites go crazy. Others get violent, commit crimes—but for pure perversion, madness, serial killings or cutters you had to stick with the whites. Packard said it was because they had centuries of inbreeding in Europe to leave their brains messed up but Push had no opinion on that. Yet it seemed to be true and so he picked Harvitt.

Daniel Harvitt. Captain with Transamerican. He went to the Jefferson County Sheriff's department and looked at a map. Harvitt lived about a mile from Rosa's house, four miles or so from the crime scene involving Linda.

He had rented a car just after noon, brought it back about six-thirty.

He ran makes on both Quintara and Harvitt. Harvitt came back squeaky clean and Quintara had a traffic citation outstanding, running a red light.

Still he took Harvitt. Daniel E. Harvitt. Age thirty-nine. Married. Two children. Straight goddam arrow—

and that's maybe why I picked him, Push thought, studying the rental form with Harvitt's name on it, studying his signature.

Cagey now—getting burned with Rosa and her husband drove him back into procedure—he called the credit card company and asked for a list of residences for eight names for the last ten years, Harvitt among them. He did not want to call attention to the one name. He told them he was trying to pin down a ring and some of these cards may have been involved.

Harvitt had lived in Cleveland, Chicago, Seattle, Atlanta and Denver. Push called the computer operator at the station and asked her to run back through the four other cities Harvitt had lived in and check for unsolved mutilation or cutter crimes, specifically those involving young women.

"Quinsey told us not to help you," Helen told him. "He says you're not working legally."

"So?"

"So it might take an hour to work all those cities— what were the names again?"

Push thanked her and hung up. Scarf brought him another beer and he paid for it.

"I'm away from work quite a few years now," Scarf said. "But if there's anything I can do to help on this Dave thing tell me and I'll do it."

"Thanks. Things are moving now. I just need a place to work to stay away from the big Q."

"You've got it."

"I'm glad you said that. I've been giving everybody

this number as my new office." He pointed up to the pay phone on the wall. "Bring me some quarters."

Scarf went to the bar, brought him a handful of quarters and went back to work.

Push took a notebook out of his pocket and wrote Harvitt's name and address in it, doodled a question mark. He wanted to work the man, close with him, see him, smell him, but that might be wrong. Especially after the abortive mess with Rosa's husband.

The pay phone rang and he answered it.

"I have a match for you." It was Melon at the forensics lab. "It's not enough to convict or even arrest or get a warrant . . ."

"But you're sure?" Push asked.

"I got a good ridge and part of a whorl on a thumb from the inside of the rubber glove—the goddam water had gotten inside the glove and ruined the rest—and a dead bang pure match from the pipe handrail in the hospital. It ain't enough of a print for court or to be legal. They need a solid portion to be admissable evidence, but I'm positive."

Oh you son of a bitch, Push thought suddenly. There in the stairwell, the door he'd heard. That was him. Harvitt. It smelled like Harvitt. "Can you check back to the crime scene for Betti Fencer—the stewardess we found up by Idaho Springs? I think there were some confused prints from that. I'm not looking for court stuff here, just some help."

"Quinsey has been here," the lab man said. "He told us to give him everything on the cutter killings—he's assigning it to someone else."

"Shit."

"So I'll keep copies of everything for you. Where is this number?"

"Scarf's. It's a bar . . ."

"I know where it is. I used to ride patrol before I went into lab work. I've been drunk more than a few times at Scarf's coming off watch. I'll get copies of these prints over there and leave them with Scarf if you're not there, also anything I find on the Betti Fencer thing. I think we got something off the backs of one of her fingernails but I can't remember for sure."

Push hung up and thought a moment. There was no way he would get any official police help on this one. Or on anything else, for that matter. Quinsey was openly cutting his legs off, hunting his head and to hell with what Push knew about the lieutenant. He couldn't get any court orders or warrants so he couldn't hit Harvitt's home for prints. But he had to get some prints from the bastard somehow—had to get close enough to him to get his thumb prints.

Oh, Christ, the car. He'd forgotten all about the car. Harvitt had rented a car and brought it back. He must have left prints in it. If he could link the car with the gloves and the stairwell he'd have Harvitt's ass.

He dropped a quarter in the telephone and called Federal Car Rental. It took him only a moment to get John Warren.

"I need to rent a car," he said after introducing himself.

"You called the right place."

"A specific car." Push looked at the papers in front

of him on the table. "It's a Ford Taurus, number CB-1302."

"I'll see if it's in." No hesitation. John, Push thought, you're going to go far young man.

"Yes. It's here. How long will you need it for?"

"A day. I want to check it for . . . marks." He held back on telling Warren about the possibility of prints.

"You've got something?"

"A smell of a smell. Nothing yet." Push lied.

"Come and get the car. Take it as long as you need. Only . . ."

"Only what?"

"If and when this comes to the press, I'd like the company's name kept out of it as much as possible."

"Done. I'll be there for the car in thirty minutes."

He hung up and called the lab. Melon answered.

"It's me. Can you get away?"

"For what?"

"I want to pick you up and take you to a car with your evidence and print kit. There's a possibility of a match with the prints you've got."

"This is quiet, right?"

"Just between us."

"I can meet you down in front of the building in thirty."

"I'm on the way."

They worked the car right in the rental parking lot. The lab man who came with Melon—his name was Racine but everybody called him Rack, because he was tall and skinny—smiled when he looked at the Ford. "Lots of flat surfaces—we might get something. If there haven't been too many in it since."

"Warren says it hasn't been rented since the crime day."

"Well, then . . ."

He used a can of spray emulsion, just a touch here and there, and an old-fashioned large magnifying glass. "Just like Dick Tracy," he mumbled as he worked. "The best is the wheel and the key but the key is usually goobered up too much. Sometimes the dash and the gear shift knob. But we're looking for the right thumb because that's what we got out of the glove. So the wheel should give us the best chance . . . ahh, see? See the son of a bitch?"

"You got something?"

He pointed to a smudge, or at least that's how it looked to Push.

"Same thumb."

"You make it definite?"

Rack frowned and looked at Melon—his boss—who nodded. "Like we said before, not for court. The handrail print was iffy at best, the glove print not usable at all and this one would let the defense run crazy. They'd have it out of court at the hearing—too smeary and ill-defined. I don't think anybody would even prosecute on this."

"But you're sure? For yourself, I mean. You're sure it's the same?"

He nodded. "Absolutely."

"Goddam," Push said. The hair went up on the back of his neck. Definite. "Goddam. It's Harvitt."

CHAPTER
EIGHTEEN

Push sat once more at Scarf's. The off watch was coming in and he would have to leave soon, before it got drunk and wild. A small patrolwoman was at the arm-wrestling stage now—beating men twice her size because she worked out in secret—and soon would be at the arm-wrestling-for-clothing-removal stage, a game she played about twice a month, and when she got all her clothes off things would go downhill fast. He could go back to his apartment or, he thought, he could sit in the street. On the best days he hated his apartment—it was a place to slow down, never stop—and on less than his best days, which was most of them, he thought of it as a warm place to shit. Besides it smelled.

On the back of one of the rental receipts he had written Harvitt's name, the words PRINTS=CAR, HOS-PITAL, RUBBER GLOVE. He thought, very briefly, of taking it to Quinsey. Asshole or not he was still a cop and Push had enough to at least set up a surveillance, if not make an arrest. He thought about laying it all out for Quinsey and asking him for help on it and in the same second dismissed the idea. Quinsey was an asshole first and cop second and he would—at the very least—turn it over to somebody else who would—at the very least—blow it and warn Harvitt, who might go underground for a year or more. Might even move. Some serial killers had killed for ten, twelve years by just going underground when the police got close, or stopping altogether for a year or so. Trails got cold, witnesses moved or died, life stopped.

No. He was alone, had to work it alone. The problem was he knew nothing, absolutely nothing about Harvitt.

He dug through his billfold and got the number for Terrenson, the psychologist, and called him from the pay phone on the wall.

"I have sort of a smell on somebody on the cutter case," Push lied. "What I need to know is if there is a way to predict when he will hit again—when or where."

"Not even if we know exactly who he is," Terrenson said. "As I said he is probably intelligent, knowledgeable, and very clever about what he does—though the act itself is completely insane. He might be on some kind of schedule that has a definite time base—once a month or something. Or it could be completely random or it may even be following a lunar cycle. That, incidentally, is fairly common."

"But there is no way to know?" Push watched as the policewoman unbuttoned her uniform shirt.

"None. All you can do is keep him under constant surveillance . . ."

Oh good, Push thought, hanging up the phone. And he's a goddam pilot and I have a fear of flying. He took the phone down again. It was happening now, cooking. He fed a quarter and called the computer room, waited.

"On those cities," she said. "Cleveland, Chicago, Seattle and Atlanta—I ran them all first looking for specific unsolved ritual killings in the last ten years and only Atlanta was negative. The other three all had cutter killings that seemed based on ritual. Three in Cleveland, one in Chicago and four in Seattle. Then I widened the parameters to include all women killed by knives but that was too open and I wound up with dozens of them, mostly apparent pimp-hooker killings. So I narrowed it down again to exclude obvious pimp-hooker killings or apparent and unsolved domestic killings that weren't necessarily ritual-based, but to include all killings where there was excessive stabbing or cutting . . ."

"You can do that?" Push asked, incredulous.

"Yes." No pride, no surprise in her voice. "We can. And the answer was a major increase. Eight in Cleveland, seven in Chicago, nine in Seattle and four in Atlanta."

Push wrote in his notebook as fast as he could, made her repeat the numbers twice and thanked her.

Jesus, he thought, looking at the list. It was like a reading of war casualties. Even if Harvitt didn't do them all, even if he'd only done half of them he was a goddam butcher.

And still, Push thought, still I know nothing about

198

him. He needed more information about the man, the way he functioned, and he kept hitting walls. He couldn't talk to his employer, Transamerican Airlines, he couldn't get warrants, he couldn't set up wiretaps, he couldn't speak to the man's family or co-workers—all methods to gain knowledge in a normal case and all methods denied to him because he didn't have enough to make a case.

Friends.

Rosa.

It came that way, just slipped into his thinking from the side. He watched the girl take a patrolman's arm down and the patrolman had to remove his shirt. Everybody laughed and drank. He had thought that Harvitt must have friends and that made him think of other pilots, their wives, parties they must go to, and there was Rosa.

He called her number. It rang six times and he was going to hang up when she answered.

"It's me," he said. "Please don't hang up."

"You're not to call here again," she said, her voice flat, like smooth, cold water. "Ever."

"I need help."

"You're about to get all the 'help' you'll ever need. My husband is turning his union loose on you . . ."

"Union?" He almost laughed. "What the hell is that?"

"The P.P.U.—the Professional Pilots Union. He's going to tell them you're harassing a pilot, using your police capacity to make illegal arrests. He is going to sue you, but he's asking them to take action as well, as an organization."

"They'll have to get in line."

"You have no idea how powerful they are. They can sue you personally and keep you running to court for the rest of your life. That's what they do when accident investigators allege pilot error in airline accidents—sue them personally. That's why so few accidents are blamed on pilot error. They're a very protective organization."

"Rosa . . ."

"Goddamit, it's over!" She was crying now. "Can't you see that? We had it out, Stephen 'understood' me, has 'forgiven' me and it's over. You go back to your goddam life and leave me alone."

"I need help," he repeated. "On the case. I know who did it, who the cutter is—the man who killed Dave—but I don't know anything about him."

"Like the last time," she said sarcastically. "Are you that sure this time? Besides, what the hell can I tell you about him?"

"He's a pilot. I thought you might know him."

"What's his name?"

"Harvitt," he said without hesitation. "Daniel Harvitt. Do you know him?"

There was stunned silence on the line. He heard her breath whistle in. "Dan Harvitt? Are you sure? How do you know it's him?"

"You know him then?" Push ignored her questions.

"Of course. Dan's family and ours are good friends. We play bridge together. Golf together. My god, Push, do you know what you're saying? This man is a leader in the community, church, a model family man. How can he be . . . what you say?"

I knew a mother once, he thought, who everybody loved, who taught Sunday school, who would never cheat on her husband, who put cigarettes out in her baby's anus. "Tell me about him."

"You can't be right. What do you have on him?"

"Tell me about him," Push repeated quietly.

She thought a moment. "I don't know what to say. Don't know what to tell you about him."

"What does he look like?"

"He's tall, good looking in an almost feminine or small boy way. Clear blue eyes, a nice smile. God, Push, he couldn't be what you say. He just couldn't."

"Can you tell me any of his habits? Does he have hobbies, anything like that?"

"He likes to garden. He has loads of flowerpots and boxes and he works on all sorts of different plants. Oh, yes, he collects things from Mexico."

"Things?"

"Like statues and sculpture. He has a whole room full of them in his house."

"Like gods—that sort of thing?" Like Aztec gods, he thought, great cutting Aztec gods who made a whole society of cutters. A whole society of blood. Shit.

"Yes. The square kind of ugly things. He's always going down to Mexico and bringing them back."

"How about his work?" He wanted to keep her talking, not give her time to become reluctant. He had a pang of conscience as he realized he was treating her like a witness, pressuring, pushing, pulling, leaning. Rosa. His Rosa and he was doing this—and he couldn't stop.

"What about it?"

"Do you know when he flies, what flights he's on?"

She sighed. "No. I don't even know what flights Stephen is on. Oh, I'll take that back. He's going to Seattle tomorrow and won't be back for two or three days."

"Stephen?"

"No. Dan. I was talking to Sue—that's his wife—and she told me he was going on a Seattle flight tomorrow and they had to service the plane so he would be laying over until it was done. That's usually one night."

Push felt it, smelled it, knew it somehow. He was going to hit again while he was in Seattle. It was all there in front of him, the list from the computer—more in Seattle than anywhere else—what the shrink had said about him being smart. He would think he was clear after doing Dave, would think they had nothing on him, had a long layover in Seattle where he'd always been safe. Maybe his favorite place to work. It had to be. Just had to be.

"Do you know his flight number?"

"No. But it leaves at eight o'clock, so it shouldn't be hard to find it."

One more question. "Do you think your husband would have told him about me? Would he know that I came out there and arrested him?"

She hesitated. "No. Stephen isn't telling anybody about that. I think he's ashamed, you know, of me. He'll have to tell the union about it when he makes out the papers but he hasn't done that yet. No. I don't think Dan could know."

There was a lot to do. He had to find the flight number, get a reservation and ticket. Go to the bank and get money. Pray. God, he hated to fly.

"I'll call you," he said. "When this is all over."

"Please," she said. "Please don't, Push."

CHAPTER
NINETEEN

He sat in seat 3A in first class on the 727 and looked at the emergency procedures card. He had chosen first class because he wanted to be close to the cockpit. He didn't ask the price, paid with plastic and hoped to god it would clear. He knew he was close to his limit.

It showed what to do if they crashed on land. All laid out in pretty pictures on the card with pretty people carefully doing as they were told. What to do if they crashed on water. What to do if the plane caught on fire. What to do if there was a hole and a "sudden loss of cabin pressure at altitude."

He put the card back in the pocket and wished they'd hurry with the booze. A plaque on the door leading to the cockpit listed the name of the captain and copilot—captain and first officer.

The captain was Daniel Harvitt.

The door to the cockpit was open and Push tried to see Harvitt's face but the angle was wrong. He had tried to sneak a look at the pilot when he boarded but the angle had been wrong then as well. The captain sat back in and around the corner to the left and it wasn't possible to see him without becoming obvious. All he could see was a short-sleeved shirt and a muscled, tanned arm with the hairs bleached blonde. The arm looked healthy. Golf-healthy. Tennis-healthy. Money-healthy.

You fucker, he thought. Sit there like you don't have a care in the world with your golden arms. You murdering son of a bitch. The arm moved around, flicked switches. He hated the arm, wanted to kill the arm.

The stewardess walked forward then, as if sensing his intensity, and closed the door to the cockpit. It locked automatically and no sooner had it locked than it opened again and Harvitt stepped out holding a small black leather square bag—the kind of bag all pilots seemed to carry.

He was wearing sunglasses so Push couldn't see his eyes. But he was good looking, as Rosa had said, well tanned and muscular. He had strong shoulders, from tennis no doubt, Push thought, hating tennis. Harvitt put the bag in the bottom of the first-class baggage bin and slid the enclosure door down until it latched. He smiled in a detached, general way at the first class section, sweeping his eyes across Push, then took a key from his pocket and unlocked the cockpit door and reentered.

In moments the jets roared, the plane backed from the loading dock, turned and made for the runway. There was no delay at the end of the runway and as soon as they turned they began the take off roll and Push was too busy to think of anything but leaving the ground, loud noise, his ass and the fact that a plane he was flying in was being piloted by a homicidal maniac.

The flight was uneventful.

The stewardess brought booze and a smile which did nothing to cheer him and he drank two small bottles of vodka and two beers in the time—about two hours—it took to fly to Seattle. Push felt slightly high as the plane approached over water—it seemed much too low to Push—to land safely.

It was dusk, close to dark. He had no plan except to follow Harvitt, watch him, wait. He went into the terminal, moved off to the side and sat in one of the soft chairs in the passenger waiting area. The vodka hit like a bomb and he fought off the fuzziness, thickness.

It seemed that Harvitt would never come and just when he thought the pilot must have gotten off the plane in some other manner the captain came walking out of the loading chute carrying the small black leather bag and a light garment bag as well. He had taken off his sunglasses and Push could see his eyes. They were blue and had the paleness around them that comes from wearing sunglasses all the time.

He walked directly past where Push was sitting and Push followed him, weaving into the people walking in the concourse.

He had trailed many times, done many stakeouts, but this was the first time he had had to do it alone, without support or backup, and he had to run to keep up.

Harvitt walked rapidly, athletically, and Push had spent the last five or six years with virtually no exercise but sex. Burritos and beer at Scarf's took their toll, as did the vodka and beer from the plane, and by the time he had followed Harvitt to the front entrance of the Seattle airport he was nearly at a dead run and had to piss so bad his teeth were floating.

Harvitt walked out the door and went directly into a cab.

Push went to the next cab in line and climbed in back.

"Follow that cab," he said to the driver.

"You're kidding, right?"

"No." Push crossed his legs and held on. "I'm not. Follow the bastard but hang back a bit." Oh god, he thought, I hope he doesn't go far.

The cabbie nodded, flicked the meter and started to drive, following as if he'd been following cabs for the last fifty years. He held back four lengths in the traffic, but stayed in the same lane as they entered a freeway and started away from the airport region.

Push was in agony from his bladder and the only thing that made it bearable was that the cabbie didn't talk. Push hated cabbies who talked. He took a lot of cabs and he hadn't learned one thing from cabbies who talked except that they could talk. This cabbie drove silently and when the cab they were following left the freeway he caught the same exit.

Harvitt pulled up to a large motel complex called the Fairview, one of those semi-posh motels where there was an average pool, average bar, poor food and the hookers ran in the hundreds. Push guessed it was an airline-furnished setup where Harvitt stayed whenever he had a layover in Seattle.

"Wait," he told the cabbie, and ran across the street to a gas station-store combination. He clawed the men's room key from the wall and ran around the outside corner at a dead lope, frantically jerked at the door and barely made it.

Fear, beer and vodka all left him at once.

Outside the cabbie was being patient. His meter was still running.

Push paid him. "How much to have you wait?"

"How long?"

"Maybe all night. I don't know. I'm following that guy in the cab."

"You some private detective or something?"

"Yeah. Like Magnum. He's playing around on his wife and I need to watch him."

"Normally, in a night like this, normally I make be-tween a hundred and fifty and two hundred dollars."

He was lying. Goddam television. Made everybody think the world was made of money. He might make eighty bucks on the best night of his life, including tips from businessmen paying for information about hookers or young boys. "I'll give you a hundred, and that includes the fare for anywhere we might have to drive if he leaves."

"One-twenty-five."

"One-ten."

"Done."

Push looked at the motel. "You saw the guy, right?"

The cabbie nodded. "Sure."

"Watch for him. I'm going to run back to that gas station and get some sandwiches and pop. I'll be right back but honk if he comes out."

"Do I get food, too?"

"Sure."

"Get me some of that turkey on white bread. They've got them there. White bread and turkey. Get me at least two of them. And some cream soda."

"Anything else?" Push said sarcastically.

"Yeah. One of those pickles sealed in plastic."

Push looked at his watch—ten o'clock local time—and trotted across to the station thinking it was going to be a long night, but he no sooner had the sandwiches and pop at the counter and had his money out than he heard the horn.

He left the food and ran out of the station, saw Harvitt getting into a cab across the street at the main entrance to the motel complex and ran to his own cab.

"He changed clothes," the cabbie said as Push slid into the back seat. "He's in slacks and a shirt. He dropped his uniform. That sucker is going out, you can bet. He's on the prowl."

You don't know the half of it, Push thought. "Hang back. We don't want to run up on him."

"I've been hacking ten years, you think I don't know how to drive?"

Push sat back. It was becoming dark and the cab

209

ahead of them seemed to be getting into heavier traffic. "Where's he heading?"

"Downtown. I would guess for Second and Pike or he might work out to Beacon Hill."

"He might look for hookers." The cutter seemed to prefer non-professionals, but he was crazy. What the hell. Who could predict crazy people? He might take an old lady now, or even a man.

No. Patterns. Stick with the patterns. He'd always used young women and he'd take a young woman now. And he might take a hooker if that's all he could get.

The cabbie nodded. "He's going for Second and Pike. He must have told the cabbie he wanted a hooker. That's where most of them are. Beacon Hill has some hooking, but it's mostly drugs. Elliot Avenue has bums but they've driven the hookers out. It'll be Pike—oh shit."

"What?" Push leaned forward.

"He's stopping and I damn near ran up on him."

"Go by, go by." Push waved him forward. "Stop past him half a block."

The cabbie pulled past Harvitt, who was out of the cab and paying his driver, and stopped near the corner. They were in an area of cheap bars, grubby motels, cruising carnivores, both male and female, and some not possible to tell. The sidewalks were crowded with them. Push got out and handed the driver a twenty.

"But you said a hundred and ten bucks!"

"That was for all night. You're done. Keep the change."

The driver swore and screeched away and Push walked from the cab to the corner, stepped around the side of a building and stood for a moment. It was like Colfax in Denver or Hennepin in Minneapolis or Sunset in Hollywood. Every city had one. Meat streets. The people were always the same. Young vicious victims. Some of the short-skirted hookers he saw Push knew couldn't be over twelve and they were raking down a hundred grand a year for their pimps. Some of the boys were younger. Ten and eleven year old boys in tight jeans, walking with all the knowledge of the world. There was the smell here, the hooker smell, the sex smell, the pervert smell—he never got used to it. Even when he worked vice. It was auto exhaust fumes and thick-hot air and some musk he did not understand but was always there on streets like this.

Cars came to the curb, pulled over, and men in suits motioned to the young girls or boys to get in the car and they, he thought, they were the real slime. The hunters. If nobody hunted there wouldn't be prey. It was the hunters who were shit.

Push stayed around the corner to avoid being seen but took a quick look from time to time. Harvitt had seen him on the plane, or at least looked towards him, and might recognize him.

The pilot was speaking to a young girl—perhaps sixteen. She was eager, had her hip cocked and young breasts jutting, but her pimp watched from a nearby car and Harvitt moved on. He was carrying a newspaper in one hand, folded over.

The knife, Push thought. He could carry it in the paper. He must have had it in his black flight bag on the plane—must have gone around security with it. I was right. He's going to hit.

He tried another girl, passed; then two more and passed; and finally crossed the street and stopped to talk to a fifth girl who loitered just beyond the corner where Push was hidden. She was white—two of the previous ones had been black—and slightly older, about seventeen. Very old for the street where nineteen was retirement age and twenty-two often meant death from overdose or assault.

Victimless crime, they called it. Push smiled. The truth was everybody involved was a goddam victim. Especially now with AIDS floating around.

The fifth girl was it.

Harvitt stayed with her, talking to her for longer than the others. Twice he looked around but Push could see no pimp or other witness watching and knew that Harvitt saw the same thing and he wondered when to take Harvitt. Too soon and he would blow it. If he was wrong and there wasn't a knife in the paper or he didn't actually catch him in the assault, catch him with some evidence, he wouldn't be able to make it stick and he knew at that instant that he wasn't going to arrest Harvitt.

Push was going to kill him.

CHAPTER
TWENTY

The realization stunned him.

It wasn't just that Harvitt pissed him off, enraged him; and it wasn't just personal because Harvitt had killed Dave. Although those two reasons were part of it. He could not look at Harvitt talking to the young hooker without rage owning him.

It was Packard.

The ghost of the old cop was always there.

"Control," Packard said. "Control is everything. If you control the situation you control the world. That's the trouble we had in Vietnam—we didn't control the situation. If there is something wrong, something going wrong, and you have a chance to make it right—that's control. That's what I do. I control things."

And here it was. If he arrested Harvitt and proceeded through normal channels the son of a bitch would skate. If he caught him with a knife stuck into a girl, caught him hacking a woman up, the son of a bitch would skate. He would get a fancy lawyer and plead insanity and spend a few years in a country club institution somewhere and he would skate. He would kill Dave and skate. He would chop up Betti Fencer and Linda Raimey and all the other girls and kill Dave and skate.

And Packard would not have called that controlling the situation and Push could not let it go by. He could not let Harvitt skate. Harvitt had to die.

Then, he thought. Then why don't I just waste the bastard now? Why wait until he does something? I know he's guilty, I know he killed Dave. Why not take him out now?

He watched Harvitt through all this. The girl was blonde—so many of them were—and almost rude the way she pushed her body out, almost militant, and Harvitt let her rub against him and seemed to stare at the top of her head, looking for something, and finally nodded and walked off with her.

Push followed on the other side of the street, weaving through a crowded stream of people. The truth was Push couldn't kill him without a reason. There was some risk of being charged—although not as much as people thought—with a bad shooting. But even in a strange city cops helped cops and he would not have trouble justifying it. Especially if Harvitt had a knife in the paper. But there was another thing stopping him, a thing he almost didn't believe; a cop thing. He needed the reason, needed the act to be able to pull the trigger. Had to have it. He couldn't kill the man in cold blood and that shocked him almost as much as knowing he had to kill Harvitt.

Standing there amidst the hookers and pimps and grifters and druggers, standing waist deep in his life he was amazed to find that any rules still held him, still guided him.

There were crib motels and a couple of ugly two-story hotels along the street in both directions and she led Harvitt finally to a doorway two and a half blocks down that opened into a darkened hallway. Harvitt had been wearing sunglasses and he took them off as he and the woman entered.

Her pimp probably had a rented apartment that he used for a crib, Push thought. Up the stairs there would be a hallway with apartments where nobody lived for more than twelve minutes. It was becoming more and more popular. Not motels but just renting a couple of rooms. That way the pimps didn't have to pay so much.

Push let them disappear up the stairs before crossing the street. His breathing was coming faster now, his pulse rate increasing. He entered the stairway, pulling his revolver as he hit the bottom step. It wasn't totally dark, some light filtered in from the street, but it was dark enough so that he almost stepped on a wino sleeping on the steps.

He swore silently, stepped around the drunk and started up the steps. At the top it leveled into a hallway, as he'd thought, but it was impossible to see much more.

There were two doorways on the left, three down the right—dark holes in a darker wall—and another door at the end of the hall.

He stood, listening, holding his breath.

Nothing.

Then he heard it. To his left, in the closest doorway, he heard a muffled sound—not a scream so much as a murmur.

He wheeled and kicked the door. It hung after the first kick and he had to kick it a second time before it blew in off the hinges and he plunged into the room, low and to the side, the handgun out in front of him held in both hands, the trigger half-squeezed.

"Police!" he yelled, to stop any action.

And it did.

On the bed was a heavy man, not obese but with a large gut. He was tied with panty hose to the four corners of the bed, nude, with an erection that was fast disappearing. He wore glasses. Standing at the foot of the bed was a young black girl—perhaps seventeen—also nude. Clearly she had been about to get on top of the man.

The man was not anything like Harvitt.

All this Push saw in the light from a cheap lamp on a pressed-wood table next to the bed, saw and registered before he could squeeze a round off. And at the same time he heard footsteps and slamming doors as the commotion warned those in other rooms and they ran.

He turned just as somebody ran past the open doorway but all he saw was movement and that it was big enough to be a man. The form disappeared down the stairs and Push wheeled and ran out the door and after him. Others were looking out doors, running—apparently every room was in use—and he had no way of knowing he was chasing the right man.

There was some light from the open room and he

could see the steps. He took them two at a time, jumping over the wino at the bottom, who was still asleep, and hit the street just as the form made it around the corner of the building to the right and disappeared down the narrow slot between the two buildings.

He followed, still at a dead run, but by the time he reached the end of the building he had lost. He ran into the alley to the rear of the apartment building but saw nothing, heard nothing.

"Damn."

He turned, holstering his handgun, and went back to the stairway.

It was empty, except for the unconscious wino, and he went back upstairs. The man who had been tied to the bed was gone—Push couldn't believe how fast he must have gotten dressed—but the black girl was still there.

"Is this a bust?" she asked. She was still nude. Her skin seemed to glow with a chocolate blackness in the light.

He shook his head. "Wrong room."

"I know all the cops working vice. How come I don't know you, sugar?"

"I'm new."

He went back into the hallway but the other rooms were empty—even the hookers were gone. He moved to the back door and saw that it was an exit that went down a rickety back stairs.

Either way. He could have gone either way.

Push stood in the darkened hallway, trying to think of what to do next, frustration sweeping over him.

He'd lost Harvitt.

Interiors
Six

It was close, so close.

That's why he didn't like to do prostitutes even when the light appeared. They were engaged in illegal work and there was always the danger of getting caught in a police raid.

As it was it did no harm—but so close!

He hadn't started with the girl—hadn't even drugged her or put the rubber gloves on—and when he heard the door in the next room slam in and the man yell "police" he'd simply run out the rear exit, down into the alley and away. Once he was a block over he signaled a cab and had it take him to Beacon Hill. He knew Beacon Hill well. He had hunted Beacon Hill before.

In its day it had been a rich community but now it was run down and given over to drugs and it was easy for him to find one. Actually there were several with the light over their heads that night. He couldn't believe how many were being given to him and he viewed it as a good omen, a sign that he was pleasing the ancient ones.

He had passed on earlier ones because the situation wasn't good. But on Beacon Hill he picked a small, Oriental girl who was working the street alone—he thought she might be Vietnamese—and they went to a place in back of an old estate where the trees and bushes were thick and she gave herself. There had been a problem because she was already on some drugs and when he gave her the Valium he gave her too much on top of the existing drugs so she died before he could perform the whole ritual. In everything he'd read it said the old ones, the gods, liked them to stay alive, not to die until it was done. It was in all the pictures of the ceremonies and even Bernal Diaz—he had studied Diaz's diaries closely—had written how important it was for them to be alive during the ritual.

But it had worked out. In the darkness in the little stand of woods he had been left alone to work and he got a major part done before she died and he had to stop because the light went out over her head.

He brought the knife and gloves with him, carefully folded in the newspaper, when he got a cab and went back to his room. There he cleaned the knife and flushed the newspaper down the toilet, tearing it in small pieces, and when that was done flushed the rubber gloves down as well, one at a time. There was blood on his hands and arms and he started to shower but when he saw himself in the mirror, the blood streaked on his lower arms, he thought of the gods and he stood for them, tall in front of the mirror, and used a finger to streak some of the blood on his forehead and chest to make him look as the gods had looked.

219

I am, he thought, I am ancient and I am new and I am what they wish me to be.

Then he showered and fell on the bed and had an hour and half to sleep until checkout time when he had to get back to the airport.

He had no dreams but it did not matter. He had done well for them. They were happy.

CHAPTER
TWENTY-ONE

Push finally went back to the motel.

He had tried to find the young hooker again, working the streets for several hours, until finally a pimp had told him—after some pressure that left Push sucking a knuckle—that the girl had been sent home after the police raid.

"You fucked my action all up," the pimp told him. "Busting the room up that way. I be a week getting my shit going again."

He had also looked for Harvitt but the pilot had run too far or gotten a cab and in the end, after covering several blocks several times so that everybody alive made him as a cop, he got a cab and went back to Harvitt's motel.

Only to miss him.

When he got to the motel it was four in the morning and he thought of setting up a watch near the gas station-convenience store across from the motel. But before doing that he went into the motel and told the desk clerk he had a message for Daniel Harvitt.

The clerk had been working on his pimples and stopped long enough to wrinkle his nose at Push—who was going now on day two in the same clothes and who had just spent several sweaty hours in a very stinking place.

"He checked out about half an hour ago," the clerk said. "They come and go at weird hours, these pilots. Come and go just anytime."

Push went to the pay phones by the entrance and called for a cab, fumed for fifteen minutes until one came, and told the cabbie to take him to the airport.

"Fast," he told the driver. "Make it fast."

"Airport. Yes. Go. Now." The driver nodded and drove off slowly, ignoring the instructions, and Push realized the cabbie knew very little English.

Push tried tapping him on the shoulder and signaling him to go faster but it didn't do any good. The cabbie just nodded again and smiled and said, "Yes. Yes. Airport."

It was after five when he got to the airport but he needn't have worried. There were no flights out for close to two hours and indeed the ticket counter for Transamerican didn't open for an hour. The security gates were closed and the only people in the lobby were a couple of street people and seven teenagers sleeping on the floor with backpacks for pillows.

Push went to the monitor screens over the counter for Transamerican and found the listing for departures.

Flight 812 left at seven-ten for Denver. He looked at his watch, an hour and a half. The pilots must have to come early to get briefed or check the weather.

He settled back on a chair next to the backpackers, watched the clock over the counter, waited. He was pulled as tight as he'd ever been, a rubber band ready to snap, but when he closed his eyes they didn't open. It was more than tired. His mother used to say she was bone-tired and he knew now what it meant. His cells, his hair, his ass was tired. An exhaustion started in the balls of his feet and went all the way into his memory and it all dumped on him when he sat down. He just couldn't make his eyes open and when he next became aware of what was happening there was a line of murmuring people at the ticket counter and it was six-thirty and he didn't have a seat yet.

There were fifteen or so people in line and he debated waiting but decided he couldn't chance it. He went to the front of the line and flashed his badge to the ticket agent, hoping she wouldn't look closely.

"Police business," he said. "I need to get a first-class ticket on flight 812 to Denver." The next person in line was a man in a three-piece suit carrying a garment bag and his eyes showed anger but settled when he saw the badge.

"First class?" She eyed him doubtfully. Not many government agencies sent their people first class.

"Yes. As fast as possible." He didn't explain anything. Stood. Waited.

She shrugged, punched some buttons on her computer, chewed her lip for a moment, then nodded. "How about 1A?"

"Sounds good."

He paid with his credit card—it was still holding—got his ticket and seat assignment and made for the security gates. He stopped there and showed his identification to avoid the metal detector as he'd done in Denver on the flight out—the rent-a-cop there was a middle-aged man who gave him a conspiratorial nod when he saw the badge and Push opened his coat to show his gun. Probably read too much Wambaugh. Probably thought of himself as a blue knight. Knew it all. All the seamy shit. Push smiled back at him. What the hell.

He found some coffee at a stand that was just opening and bought three cups. He drank two as fast as he could as he walked to the loading gate—it was only six gates down the concourse after the security—and let the caffeine jolt him awake. The third he sipped in the gate area, sitting in one of the plastic molded chairs.

He had no idea what to do. He had blown the tail but it was an honest mistake. If it had been the right room and Harvitt had been cutting up the girl it would have worked out right. He thought of calling the Seattle police and seeing if there was a victim but he suspected there wasn't; that the incident in the old hotel with the hooker had caused Harvitt simply to work his way back to the motel and drop it for the time being.

And now he did not know what to do.

Stay on the son of a bitch. That's all he could think of—stay on him day and night until he hit again. Stay on him until he could get something to have him with, make him act and then kill the bastard.

Some plan, he thought. Some goddam plan.

He was tired. Strung out and tired and didn't know what to think or do. They called for first-class boarding and he went down the tube and onto the plane.

The plaque still read DANIEL HARVITT and he found his seat. It was on the right and he could see into the cockpit through the open door and again he saw Harvitt's arm, the side of his head moving as he performed preflight checks. The arm floating gracefully up to overhead switches, down to others on the control column, the dash, back up in the swinging movements of the preflight—the cutter's arm.

People came on the plane, walked past him back into the coach section and he sat, sipping a coffee the attendant had given him, and Harvitt suddenly appeared before him.

It was that sudden. He took a sip of coffee, smelling himself—two days and more running in stink and sweat and his clothes were growing to him—and he looked up and Harvitt was looking directly into his eyes. The pilot had a paper in one hand that he was placing in his flight bag in the baggage compartment and he had turned his head and was studying Push.

Push's first thought was: he made me.

The pilot wasn't wearing sunglasses and was looking intently, almost staring at Push. There was something there, something alive between them, and Push realized that it wasn't that Harvitt was looking at him so much as he was looking in him. He was seeing something inside Push, something Push didn't even know was there, some mad thing, and Push knew then that he wasn't just made, his cover wasn't just blown, he was marked with it.

Push smiled. Not with humor, but with recognition, and he was about to shove him, about to drive him over the edge, about to tell him he'd seen Harvitt with the girl and watch his reaction, when the pilot turned abruptly and reentered the cockpit.

It was over so fast, had happened so fast that Push almost didn't believe it had happened at all.

The passengers finished loading, the cockpit door closed and locked, the plane pulsed and roared to life and moved away from the terminal while the flight attendant told him about emergency procedures and Push sat there, all the while staring at the closed door of the cockpit, wondering if Harvitt meant anything by the look.

Interiors
Seven

The light.

The final light of all the lights there were had come to him.

At first he thought the man's face had been familiar, then he knew, recognized him from the flight out of Denver, remembered seeing him across from the motel as he got into a cab and knew him for what he was—a policeman. He was ragged looking and had a cheap suit and smelled and had the thick neck and shoulders so many policemen seemed to have. It had not been a general vice raid on the cheap hotel but this man, this policeman. It was not hard to figure out and he had a moment of panic, a part of a moment, because he thought the police must know something to have a man follow him but knew then they would have done something if they truly knew.

They would have arrested him or stopped him and he had a second or so of exultation, triumph, when he realized he had performed the ritual under the very eyes of the authorities; while this man was watching him, or trying to watch him, he had taken a chosen one for the gods and done it almost perfectly and they had not been able to stop him. They could never stop him.

He had been protected.

Then he saw the light. It started over the policeman's face, in his face and over his head and there was glory in it and newness because he had never, not once, seen the light on a man; always it had been women. But the light grew, flew out and out of the policeman until it filled the first-class section, warped and turned and filled and billowed in glory and gold until the whole plane glowed with a beautiful soft light and he knew why he had been selected, why he had been protected and guided.

It wasn't luck. Had nothing to do with chance.

He was under their special protection because they had watched him, watched him through Cleveland and Atlanta and Chicago and Denver and knew of his loyalty, knew that he was unique, knew that of all the princes he alone was perfect because he alone was in this position.

Only he would have this opportunity.

It was why he had been chosen, why he was the chosen one, why they made him a prince.

Only he could make the supreme, the ultimate sacrifice.

And he set the autopilot and turned to his copilot when they reached cruising altitude and leveled, got on the step where the plane seemed to be perpetually flying downhill, turned to him and told him he felt a strange vibration in the tail section, ordered him to check the tail assembly and make certain everything was correct in the cable housing and actuators back there. The copilot looked at him strangely but rose and left the cockpit because copilots did not question captain's orders and he locked the door as the copilot left, locked and pushed the deadbolt on the inside.

And was alone.

They had left much of it to him. He knew what they wanted, but the details were left to him and he was honored by that. Honored that they trusted him. They would want the maximum. They always wanted the maximum and he thought at first of a mountain. To hit a mountain at full cruising speed would furnish them with the maximum effect.

Then he thought of the temple. They liked temples and ordered the priests to tell the princes of Mexico to build huge temples just for the ritual. He had often constructed small altars when he performed the ritual just to give at least the feeling of a temple. To give them that, to give them not only the supreme sacrifice but a temple as well, would assure him a place at their sides for all eternity.

And there was a temple.

Just to the right of their flight path lay Salt Lake City.

And the Mormon Temple.

It was perfect.

He tweaked the autopilot to bring the compass heading around to the altered course that would lead it to Salt Lake City, and looked at his watch. At this speed and having reached altitude it would be about fourteen minutes. The plane banked and moved around to the right a small amount, assumed the new heading and settled, and he leaned back in the seat and put his hands on the armrests and stared out the window, completely at peace, resting, waiting for the moment when he would take it out of autopilot and begin the descent into Salt Lake City.

CHAPTER
TWENTY-TWO

Push saw the copilot leave the cockpit and walk back through the first-class section towards the tail.

In two minutes he was back. He took a key out of his pocket and put it in the door to the cockpit, tried it, pulled on it, wiggled it.

The door didn't open.

Push put his cup down. Hairs started to lift on the back of his neck though he didn't know for certain why yet. Across the aisle to his left a woman sipped a martini. She was wearing a cotton dress with flowers printed on it and he saw each flower with bright clarity. He smelled a new smell coming from his body and knew it was fear. Goddam planes.

The copilot knocked on the cabin door. Waited. He looked like all pilots looked to Push, even Harvitt. Assured, healthy, suntanned, balanced and thoughtful. He was perhaps thirty-five with reddish blonde hair and green eyes and would look thirty-five when he was fifty.

Nothing happened.

He gave a perplexed look to the first-class stewardess standing next to him in the gallery, mixing a drink, and shrugged. Next to the cockpit door hung a white phone and the copilot took it down and punched a number into the pushbuttons in the handle. Put the receiver to his ear. Waited.

Push felt his stomach tighten, his ass pinch.

Nothing happened.

The copilot hung the phone up, took it down and punched the number again, put it to his ear. Waited. He said something into the phone but turned away so Push couldn't quite hear it. Push thought he said "Captain Harvitt," but couldn't be sure. The copilot now had a mild look of concern on his face as he listened on the phone for an answer.

Nothing happened.

He hung the phone up, tried his key again in the door and used more strength, half bending the key in the lock and jerking the door back and forth in its frame.

"He's pushed the deadbolt into place," the copilot said to the stewardess, loud enough for Push to hear it. Both the copilot and the stewardess now had an openly worried look.

The son of a bitch has gone over, Push thought; that's what the look meant. He's cracked. He made me and it drove him over the edge. He took his seat belt off and stood, approached them.

"Please, sir." The stewardess held her hand up. "Please return to your seat . . ."

Push ignored her, took his badge out of his coat pocket and let both of them see it without showing it to the rest of the cabin.

"Into the galley," he said. "We have to talk. Now."

The three of them crowded into the small galley alcove and Push used his body to block the entry to keep any sound from escaping.

"I'm a homicide detective in Denver," he said, leaning close and trying to whisper, though the roar of the engines made it hard. "I have been investigating your captain," he tried to make his voice sound official, "and have reason to believe he is a . . . serial killer." He had started to say cutter but changed it at the last moment.

Both of them stared in open disbelief.

"Dan Harvitt?" The copilot shook his head. "Not possible."

"It's not only possible but definitely true. Now, I think he recognized me and has locked you out of the cockpit . . ."

"Jesus, man," the copilot stopped him. "You're talking about the captain of this airliner."

"Has locked you out of the cockpit," Push repeated, "and plans to do something drastic."

"What?"

"I don't know. Something. Or he wouldn't have locked you out. I think there is great danger and if we don't get him out of the cockpit we may all die."

It's like a manual, he thought—I sound like a goddam manual.

The copilot shook his head and moved around Push,

out of the galley. "You're crazy. Maybe he just didn't hear me . . ."

He pounded on the door again and when nothing happened reached for the white phone. "Captain, this is Wilson. There seems to be a problem with the door. Please open it."

Push turned to the first-class baggage compartment and opened the shutter door. He found Harvitt's black case and opened it, began rummaging in it.

"Sir?" The stewardess put her hand on his arm. "You can't be in there. That's Captain Harvitt's private material . . ."

Push grunted and pulled out a rigid black case, much like a flute case. He opened it and the knife lay there. It was long, with a narrow blade, and a black hard rubber handle with a checkered pattern.

He knew exactly what it was because he had once had a brief affair—three days—with a woman studying to be a doctor and she'd owned a knife exactly like it. It was a surgical knife from the Civil War era. The woman had used it for carving roasts. A joke. Push had not laughed.

The knife looked somehow evil. The blade was nine or ten inches long and tapered and curved down to a point and had been polished so much it was almost like chrome or burnished silver. It was designed for gross amputations—as the woman described it—the heavy, meaty part of arms and legs. She had shown him the quick, surgical cut to the bone before the small saw could be used, using the roast to illustrate it. He couldn't eat it.

He showed the copilot and stewardess the knife, still

hiding it from the other passengers. "This is what he used . . ."

He grabbed the phone from the copilot, put it to his ear. "Harvitt, listen, this is the police. We know about you. It's all right. You just need help. Open the door now and we'll help you." Lying came so easy for him. "Just open the door and we'll do all we can to help you . . ."

"Can he hear me at all?" Push asked the copilot.

"Yes. If he has the headset on." Wilson rubbed the back of his neck, looked almost embarrassed. "Look, if you're right, and I do mean if—I just can't believe it."

"Believe it."

"So if you're right, what do you think he means to do?"

Push shook his head. "Your guess is as good as mine. Anything. Crash the plane. Kill us all. He's whacko. We have to get him out of there. Now." And he almost added: one way or the other.

Packard's rule of control. Never let the suspect control the situation. Maintain control. Talk about losing control, Push thought. Christ. "Move all these people out of first class," he told the stewardess, "back into the other cabin, and close the drapes again."

She looked at the copilot who nodded and she left to do it. By now the people in first class knew something was wrong and the worry had spread magically to the rear compartment. Passengers stopped her, asked for an explanation. Murmurs went up and back the main cabin, growing in sound, and she stuck her head through the curtain. "If you don't need me up there I'd better stay back here with them and help the other attendant."

Push nodded and as soon as her head disappeared he pulled out his revolver, aimed where the bolts came through the door to hold the deadbolt in place.

The copilot shook his head. "No shooting. If you puncture the hull it could cause an explosion as the cabin depressurized . . ."

"Like the one over Hawaii?" Push had a mental image of the plane from pictures on television, the huge hole in the fuselage.

"Yes. No shooting."

He still had the knife. He put the revolver away and worked the knife into the crack between the door. It was at best a flimsy door but it was seated well and he couldn't get the blade through the opening.

"I'll have to break it down. Explain to me, exactly, how he's sitting."

"He'll be in the left seat. He'll probably be wearing his shoulder harness and you'll have to release it. There's a release button in the center of his chest. Just rotate it counterclockwise and it will let the harness straps loose. Then try to get him out of the seat as fast as you can, before he can do anything, and I'll try to get into the other seat as fast as I can to take control of the pla . . ."

Suddenly the plane pitched forward and increased speed. The maneuver was so sharp it threw Push up against the ceiling, crammed his head into the corner and drove the copilot up next to him. People in the main cabin screamed. Out of the corner of his eye Push saw one of the stewardesses and several unbelted passengers slammed up against the ceiling. Trays of food and drinks flew up and splattered against the ceiling, clattered back down to the floor.

"He's taking her down!" The copilot yelled, though his mouth was right next to Push's ear. "He's going to crash her!"

As the plane assumed the down angle Push and the copilot fell to the floor. But the floor was still pitched down radically.

"He can't hold her like this much longer," the copilot yelled. "The speed is increasing too much. It'll break apart."

Frantically Push kicked at the door. It didn't give. He pulled back and kicked again and again, terror driving him now, but still it didn't let go. He pulled himself back, away from the door to the rear of the first-class compartment, took a breath, gathered his legs beneath him and with all the strength he could find powered himself down and into the door.

"Arrrrrhhhhhhnnnngh!"

It gave.

He blew into the cabin on the scream, the door slamming ahead of him.

Harvitt half turned his head when Push hit him. The windshield showed no sky, only earth. A city. He was aimed at the center of a city.

Push reached over Harvitt's shoulder and clawed for the release on his harness. Pulled at and turned everything he could grab, screaming obscenities now, over and over.

"Fuckerfuckerfuckerfucker . . ."

The roaring engines mixed with the terror that came from seeing the ground come at the plane. He ripped and tore at the pilot's chest, felt Harvitt striking at him, at his head, and felt him come loose, felt the release of the harness suddenly give. He grabbed the pilot's tie and hair and pulled, raw panic powering him now, and he dragged and screamed and clawed Harvitt out of the seat, Harvitt kicking and ripping at his face, biting and trying to scream through the choking tie. Both animals now, he dragged the pilot up and out of the seat and up through the cockpit into the first-class cabin.

"Fuckerfuckerfuckerfucker."

Nothing could stop him. He pulled at Harvitt, ignored the bites and scratches, ignored the blood dripping from his face, and jammed Harvitt under the first row of seats, jammed his head in and twisted the tie, pulled and twisted and knew nothing else; did not feel or see the copilot fight by him, did not feel or see the plane level just above the streets of Salt Lake City, did not feel or see the stewardess pulling at him, dragging at his coat, his hair. Felt only the tie and his own wild lust as he twisted and pulled and heaved until Harvitt's arms stopped moving, until Harvitt's legs quit kicking, until he could smell Harvitt's bowels release and knew, finally, that Harvitt was dead.

Then he fell sideways to lie on the floor next to the dead pilot, crying, and only after a moment did he realize he was no longer screaming obscenities but saying, "Dave, Dave, Dave . . ."

And knew, finally, it was over.

Epilogue

Push sat at his desk and picked at his facial scabs. Two of the bites had become infected and he'd had to have antibiotics for them but they were healing nicely now.

Everything was healing nicely now.

The shit had largely already hit the fan and been dissipated. Quinsey had done his worst but the prints from the knife and the crime scenes and gloves had been enough to shut him up, even though there still wasn't enough to make a case. There was of course no case necessary. Harvitt's actions—trying to crash into Salt Lake City—had made him obviously insane and, as final proof, the toilet in Harvitt's motel room in Seattle had plugged on a rubber glove. The maid used a plunger to get it out and was about to throw it away when she saw blood inside one finger and decided to tell her boyfriend who had heard about an illegal abortion ring. They told the police who then tested the blood found in the glove against the blood from the Oriental girl they had found on Beacon Hill. It was a match and so everything had been smoothed over. The airline didn't want the bad publicity of having a maniac for a pilot, Quinsey wanted to be able to take credit for "his" work in solving the cutter crimes, and Push wanted to be left alone.

Everybody got what he wanted.

Except that Push now had a mountain of paperwork and it was a warm summer day and he didn't want to be sitting on his ass at his desk.

"Are you Detective Edward Tincker?"

Standing in front of him was a man in a tee shirt. On the front of the tee shirt was the name of a rock group. The man was pushing thirty, but he dressed young and was smiling and looked pleased with himself.

Push nodded. "I am. What do you want?"

"I wanted to give you this."

He handed Push some paper, turned and walked away. Push looked in his hand and saw it was a summons. For a civil action against him by the Professional Pilots Union. For ". . . harassment and annoyance" of ". . . one of its members, herein named Stephen P. Baylor."

Well shit, he thought, I wonder what *P* stands for?

He stood and threw the summons in the wastebasket. He would go to Scarf's and drink six or seven dark, cold beers as fast as he could, thinking of Dave while he drank them. Then he would eat a burrito. Then he would drink some more and get drunk and when he was drunk he would drive by his ex-wife's place, just for the hell of it, and then he would call Rosa and tell her he loved her and maybe she could meet him and they could go to a motel and get all sweaty-belly.

Because that's what hot afternoons were for.

ABOUT THE AUTHOR

GARY PAULSEN has spent fourteen years researching a crime trilogy, of which *Night Rituals* is the first book. Paulsen, an award winning writer whose hobbies include long-distance dog sledding, has twice run the Iditarod in Alaska. His novel *Murphy,* which was built around an early crime in the old West, was used as evidence to help convict an actual serial killer in Minneapolis. Mr. Paulsen makes his home in Becida, Minnesota, with his wife and son.

Now there are two great ways to catch up with your favorite thrillers

Audio: _____

DON'T MISS
THESE CURRENT
Bantam Bestsellers

☐	28390	**THE AMATEUR** Robert Littell	$4.95
☐	28525	**THE DEBRIEFING** Robert Littell	$4.95
☐	28362	**COREY LANE** Norman Zollinger	$4.50
☐	27636	**PASSAGE TO QUIVIRA** Norman Zollinger	$4.50
☐	27759	**RIDER TO CIBOLA** Norman Zollinger	$3.95
☐	27811	**DOCTORS** Erich Segal	$5.95
☐	28179	**TREVAYNE** Robert Ludlum	$5.95
☐	27807	**PARTNERS** John Martel	$4.95
☐	28058	**EVA LUNA** Isabel Allende	$4.95
☐	27597	**THE BONFIRE OF THE VANITIES** Tom Wolfe	$5.95
☐	27510	**THE BUTCHER'S THEATER** Jonathan Kellerman	$4.95
☐	27800	**THE ICARUS AGENDA** Robert Ludlum	$5.95
☐	27891	**PEOPLE LIKE US** Dominick Dunne	$4.95
☐	27953	**TO BE THE BEST** Barbara Taylor Bradford	$5.95
☐	26892	**THE GREAT SANTINI** Pat Conroy	$5.95
☐	26574	**SACRED SINS** Nora Roberts	$3.95
☐	28436	**PAYMENT IN BLOOD** Elizabeth George	$4.95

Buy them at your local bookstore or use this page to order.

Bantam Books, Dept. FB, 414 East Golf Road, Des Plaines, IL 60016

Please send me the items I have checked above. I am enclosing $_____
(please add $2.00 to cover postage and handling). Send check or money
order, no cash or C.O.D.s please.

Mr/Ms _____

Address _____

City/State _____ Zip _____

FB—10/90

Please allow four to six weeks for delivery.
Prices and availability subject to change without notice.